STELFOX STREET

STELFOX STREET

Short Stories

MARGARET SLAVEN

authorHOUSE®

AuthorHouse™
1663 Liberty Drive
Bloomington, IN 47403
www.authorhouse.com
Phone: 1-800-839-8640

First published by AuthorHouse   10/05/2011

ISBN: 978-1-4670-4090-7 (sc)
ISBN: 978-1-4670-4089-1 (ebk)

CONTENTS

Acknowledgements vii

Forward ix

I Want my Children 1

Chucky 7

Grief 15

Get Used to It 19

The Samaritan 25

The Korean 29

A Day in the Country 35

The Piano Teacher 43

Someday You'll Understand 47

Be Careful What You Wish For 49

Faith and Hope 57

I'm Sending You an Angel 61

Make Believe 67

The Shining Star 73

Perils and Dangers 77

Crossing the Street 81

This is not a Party 87

ACKNOWLEDGEMENTS

S HORT STORIES should be the easiest of literary forms to work in. The drain on imagery and feelings, which a poem demands, is lighter; there is less weaving and sustaining of plot elements, which occur in a novel; and opinion, so vital to an essay, may be omitted. Of course, the "should" in that first sentence is the tip-off. Characters in short stories, in order to be meaningful, have to be painted in quick, strong strokes; and the plot tolerates no rambling from the main track. I'm not sure if my stories meet this criteria, but if they do, or even approach it, it's because they were nudged along by Barry Sheinkopf, from whose writing classes I emerged, believing in my ability to create. Thank you, Barry, and my thanks also goes to my sister Adelaide Kern and my friend Bonnie Kreielsheimer, who read many of the stories and offered apt suggestions and helpful comments. However, all of the stories would still be sitting in my computer, if it weren't for the skill of my son Sterne, who patiently (okay, sometimes not so patiently) rounded them up for submission to the publishing process. Not only do I owe him my heartfelt thanks for doing this, but also for creating the hands-down best short story book cover. Thanks to Adelaide, Bonnie, Barry, and Sterne. And, while I have this opportunity, thanks to my family and friends for their care and support.

FORWARD

D OG WALKING can be a meditative exercise. The dog lopes along, pausing often to sniff and graze, allowing the person at the other end of the leash to wander with her thoughts, which might be anything from a grocery list to the great American novel. One late autumn evening I was walking a few blocks from home with Shane, the family's Springer, thinking about a subject for a short story I wanted to write. In a corner yard I noticed a woman kneeling near the fence that wrapped around her property. It was an odd time for gardening, and what she was doing seemed odd—carefully placing clam shells in the dirt, outlining the yard's border. Perhaps not an unusual landscape touch at the Jersey Shore or on Cape Cod, but I wanted to tell her it wasn't practical in northern New Jersey, where the shells would get muddier with each successive rainfall, making her effort a vain one. Of course, I didn't tell her. As I continued walking that evening, wondering about the woman's life and why she was outside at dinner time, kneeling on the cold ground, I knew I had something I wanted to write about. From that story, "I Want My Children," came others, stories existing for me behind the windows and doors of houses along the streets Shane and I walked. I named the street Stelfox, and these are my stories . . .

I WANT MY CHILDREN

MURRAY RUMSFELD was more discomfited than surprised by the news of his daughter's latest break with reality.

"Back in the hospital?" he replied when Myra, his wife, called him on a windy afternoon in late autumn. "What about Joshua, where is he?"

All the details and loose ends would have to be attended to, and Henry was no help, his husbandly status having long since ceased to be anything but titular. It would be up to Murray and, of course, Myra, to keep Ruthie's household, such as it was, up and running. And it was no surprise that his daughter had had to be taken, tied to a gurney and shrieking obscenities, from her home, since he knew that Ruthie without her medication always ended up in one hospital or another. He hated the thought of driving to Jersey, but he'd have to do it. They couldn't leave Josh alone.

An hour later Murray nosed the wide, blunt front end of the Buick to the curb in front of the small house Ruthie and Henry had purchased when they learned they were going to have a baby. That had been a happy time, schizophrenia only a word you'd sometimes see in <u>Time</u> magazine under 'Medicine,' not a disease capable of sucking a life worth living out of your daughter.

Nearly dark already at five in the afternoon; lights shone from the front windows. He eased his heavy frame out of the car and stood a moment, gazing up and down the street. The old man halfway down the block was out raking, but he was always out there chasing every stray leaf. Otherwise, nobody peeking from behind drawn shades, no kids lining the sidewalk, pointing toward the house and snickering. Not as bad as he had feared.

The path to the house was lined with sea shells, as was the perimeter of the lawn, outlining nonexistent flower beds. Ruthie's work. Took her weeks of kneeling and placing just so, the gray, lusterless clam shells. Would have made sense in a house at the shore, but in suburban New Jersey . . . well, that was Ruthie.

She had seemed your average child. Met Henry when she was nineteen, married a year or so later. It was after Josh was born that the strangeness started. She wouldn't take Josh out for walks in the carriage as most women do—something about getting germs. At first they'd thought she was just being fussy, like some new mothers are, but instead of relaxing as Josh got older, she got more and more peculiar. Ruthie's Rules, they'd called them. Wash your hands before you touch the baby was one of them, one they smiled about, but the smiles faded as the rules multiplied like cancer cells: wash your hands before you change the baby's diaper, before you pick up a toy, lower the side of the crib, touch the door frame to the baby's room. "Your daughter's way of controlling her environment," one doctor told them.

The front door was locked. Murray jiggled the doorknob, then jabbed the bell. Joshua let him in, Joshua with eyes too old for his eight year-old face and hands that were never still.

"Hey, pal. Locking your old granddad out?"

"Granddad, you hear about Mommy?"

Murray pulled the boy to him and gave the thin shoulders a hug. "Yeah, Grandma called me. She'll be okay, son. She'll be back."

"Grandma says she's going to stay with me. Are you staying?"

"We'll see. Where's Grandma?"

"Upstairs." The boy wandered back to his spot on the carpet in front of the TV.

Murray took the steps slowly. The house had a musty, unpleasant odor, like an old person's. Ruthie refused to open windows, and her obsession with cleanliness had dwindled to sporadic bouts with the vacuum cleaner.

He found Myra scrubbing the walls in Ruthie's bedroom.

"What the hell?" Murray stared at the walls. Foot-high writing had cascaded down all four of them, the black letters spelling out what read to him like passages from the Torah.

Myra wrung out the sponge she was using, into the pail at her feet. "She's really bad this time, Murray, really bad." Her words were steeped in despair, not put out as some sort of explanation or update.

He went over to her and took the sponge out of her hand. "This isn't working, Myra. She must have used permanent ink. Come on, let's get something to eat. Then I'll drive over to the hospital, see what's what." He slid a hand around her shoulders and turned her toward the doorway.

In the kitchen she put the tea kettle on the stove and turned to a sink overflowing with food-caked dishes and pans. Murray knew he should help, push aside the hopelessness that was filling his gut like acid and grab a towel, dry the dishes as she tried to bring some order to the confusion. But he collapsed on a chair at the table, put his elbows on the newspapers that covered it, and dropped his head into his hands.

"I left a message on Henry's voice mail," Myra said.

Henry had gotten lost amid Ruthie's rules was how Murray saw it. He went to the office early, stayed late, and worked weekends. He had tried at first, Murray granted him that. When one idiot doctor told him to get Ruthie pregnant—his thinking being that she would lighten up once a second baby arrived—Henry had complied. Well . . . Ruthie's miscarriage had sent her right over the crumbling edge. To this day she referred to 'Susan' as among the living—Susan, the nonexistent second child. Murray pushed his glasses to the top of his head and rubbed his eyes. It was a miracle Josh hadn't been driven nuts by all the craziness that went on in the house.

"No answer, I take it," Murray said, "from Henry."

"Not yet." She bent over the sink, lost in the steam from the faucet. "I'm thinking we should take Joshua home with us, Murray."

Murray looked up. They had talked about taking Josh, because that's what it would amount to, taking him to Queens on a permanent basis. They'd always backed off, knowing what it would do to Ruthie. And, he had to admit, knowing what it would do to them. They weren't getting any younger, God knew. Raising a kid was a big responsibility, and what sort of life would Josh have, living with two old folks? But what sort of life did he have now? And that's where they always left it, bouncing back and forth between those two questions; in the meantime Josh stayed with a mother who fooled around with her medicine, so that she had progressed from being troubled to the black hole of paranoia.

"You think so?" he asked.

She dunked a skillet into the soapy water in the sink and pushed a stray strand of hair off her forehead with the back of her free hand.

"We keep thinking every time is going to be the last, and we're kidding ourselves, Murray. Ruthie's getting worse, not better." Her voice was hard now; she'd succeeded in putting aside the despair. "We leave him here with a practically nonexistent father, he's going to have his own nervous breakdown." She sighed. "I don't know, it just seems like the time has come to take the bull by the horns, to act. Do you know what I mean?" She turned, soapsuds dripping from her hands, and looked over at him.

"Think about it. I'll get us dinner." She paused, gazing at the mess that was Ruthie's kitchen. "Or maybe you could get us a pizza. Josh would like that, I bet."

After making a call to the local pizzeria, Murray returned to the table and began to clear it. "We'd be taking him away from his friends, the neighborhood. Here he can go next door or across the street and get away from it. They seem like nice normal families. He'd miss that."

"I don't know, Murray, I don't know how normal any of us is." She handed him place mats and napkins.

"What happened today?" he asked, not really wanting to know the details, hoping Myra would brush aside his question with an, "Oh, the usual nonsense," sort of reply.

But she said, "Ruthie called the school, demanded they send Josh and Susan home, that there were secret agents in their classrooms, that they had orders to harm the children. 'I want my children!' she'd screamed, 'I want my children!'" Myra took a trembling breath and went on, "The principal had my number as the person to call in an emergency, and, thank God, he figured it was an emergency."

Myra broached the idea to Josh about going to Queens, while they ate.

"You mean stay at your house tonight? What did Daddy say?" With his front teeth Josh tugged at the rubbery slice of pizza.

Murray couldn't tell if the boy was pleased at the idea or reluctant about leaving home. And he noticed the 'tonight.' They'd have to cope with the permanence of the deal later, once they had him settled in Queens.

"We haven't talked about it with your dad yet," Murray said, "but he has to be going to work every day, Josh, so maybe it would be good if you stayed with us."

Later, Murray remembered that he hadn't added "'until your mom gets home," as he had in the past. And he was glad for that instance of honesty.

THE END

CHUCKY

"**I**s it too much to ask for a pitcher of milk on the table?" Eliot frowned at the litter of breakfast confusion spread before him. His voice approached a whine.

"Right there," Nancy indicated with a nod of her head. She stood at the sink, rinsing the children's sugar-coated cereal bowls. Her hands, encased in pink rubber, dripped suds into the sink. "There beside the Cheerios box."

Eliot stared. "A cow? You're serving milk in a cow?"

"It's a pitcher, El." She shed the gloves and picked up the white china cow pitcher to demonstrate. "See, the milk comes out her mouth and her tail is the handle. I think it's cute," she said, laying a finger gently on the cow's head.

"'Cute' is a kid's word, Nancy."

A Miniature Schnauzer stepped from his basket in the corner and carefully stretched his chubby length before trotting across the kitchen floor. The sound of his nails on the tiles reminded Nancy of the littlest Billy Goat Gruff, the one that trip-tropped across the troll's bridge. Staring up at Eliot, or rather, at Eliot's hand holding the toast, the dog sat, his front paws leaving the floor in slow motion until they were chest level, a pose he held until the last bite disappeared into Eliot's mouth. Only then did the paws return to the floor. With a puff of resignation, the dog trip-tropped back to his basket.

When the front door closed behind Eliot, Nancy, pausing briefly to admire the dining room table set with the best china for lunch, took the stairs to the second floor two at a time. The girls' room required little attention—a comforter straightened, a window shade raised. The door to Chucky's room was closed, a Do Not Disturb sign prominently displayed. She pushed the door open, her nose wrinkling at the strong little boy smell. The room was a rabbit warren of paper, metal, and plastic in various stages of construction.

Placing each foot with care, Nancy made her way to a window to admit a stream of chilled air before confronting the bed. Sheets, blanket, and pillow were jumbled into a puzzle, a daily challenge. Methodically she worked her way down to the mattress cover before reassembling the parts until the bed stood pristine in the surrounding disarray. Once the upstairs had been put to rights, she returned to the kitchen for her bag and car keys. The dog emerged from the basket and bowed before her, stubby tail wagging an invitation to play.

"Sweetie-love," Nancy crooned, bending over and rubbing the curly head, "Mummy has to get the flowers for her bridge club luncheon. You guard the house, that's my brave boy."

She drove along pleasant residential streets whose curbs were obscured by mounds of dry leaves. Passing an elementary school, she noted with approval its windows decorated with paper ghosts, witches, and pumpkins, some probably the work of her daughters, who at this very moment were sitting at their desks inside two of the school's large, sunny classrooms. Nancy loved to visit the school, to walk down halls redolent of wax and chalk and the fresh fruit of mid-morning snacks. The teachers wore skirts or neat slacks and were addressed as Mrs., Ms, or Mr. The principal, Dr. Sherman, portly in his middle-age, dropped in on the classes like a benevolent uncle, to teach the children obscure facts about a president or the correct spelling of 'picnicking' before withdrawing to his paneled corner office.

The director of Chucky's school didn't have an office. She sat at a scarred desk in a niche in the hall. How many schools had Chucky attended? Nancy wondered. Maybe five, if she counted the preschool years. Five and not one in a real school building. Chucky's schools were in church halls or community centers, his teachers wore jeans and out-size cardigans and were called Lisa and Tammy and the like. Not Mrs. Karas, of course, but she was the exception. She had experience. That was why she'd been able to manage Chucky.

"Today, today is, today is Thursday, right? Today is Thursday and yesterday, what was yesterday? Rita? Yesterday was . . . come on, Rita, you know what yesterday was. If today is Thursday, yesterday was . . . Wednesday! Right, ooh, good, Rita, good work." Laurie Michaels took time to smile her pleasure on Rita before continuing. "And if today is Thursday, what will tomorrow be, Ian? Tomorrow will be . . . you can say it, tomorrow will be . . ."

Chucky watched his fingers as they traveled through the space between his chair and Amanda Gold's chair, Laurie's chanting filling his ears with the day's calendar exercise. Calendar. Calendar for retards, Chucky thought. His fingers, out of Laurie's line of vision, crept toward Amanda's pretty skirt. Chucky's eyes tracked his fingers, closer to the softness. What to do but watch them move, closer, closer.

"All right, we're batting a thousand this morning, let's keep it going. Tomorrow will be Friday, good, Ian. Now, for the day's date. Today is Thursday the . . . ? Who knows—"

"STOP IT! Make him stop it!" Amanda's chair crashed backward as she leaped to her feet. "Chucky's doing it, Laurie! Make him stop touching me!" The hysteria in her cries ran through the children like an electric shock, snaking whip-like around the circle. Rocking, giggling, spinning, the group of eight children exploded from the circle of chairs. The day's opening exercise lay in shambles.

The tiny gold anchor pin rode Nancy's left breast with aplomb. She leaned over the counter and signed her name at the bottom of the bill. Handing the pen back to the florist, she took the chrysanthemum centerpiece, nestled in the cardboard box he held out to her.

"Enjoy your party, Mrs. Christmas." He smiled his appreciation of her trade, admiring both breast and anchor.

"Chucky," Laurie called, "careful where you're walking." But Chucky took an extra-long step and brought his untied sneaker down on Jennie's heel. The resulting commotion delayed the class exodus from the playground, which was just fine with Chucky. He preferred outdoors. He liked watching the clouds, the way they looked like mounds of mashed potatoes. He liked the way the sunshine sparkled on the hairs on his arms. Anyhow, reading waited in the classroom. He hated reading all those words. He could never remember any of them.

"Watch my finger, Chucky, keep your eyes on the word," Laurie would plead, turning his chin toward the open book on the desk in front of them.

They thought he could control his eyes, make them look into their eyes, keep them from moving sideways, downways. Well, he couldn't. He wasn't in charge of his eyes, just like he wasn't in charge of his fingers, reaching out, touching the children, digging into Popcorn.

Popcorn had been his dog once, his birthday present, all wound up in a blue ribbon. He'd held Popcorn tight, felt his balloon shape, smelled his wooly smell, heard his puppy cries. Mommy had pulled open his fingers and taken the puppy and said she'd take him 'til Chucky was old enough to 'proper care' him.

He didn't know what 'proper care' was.

Then she'd named the puppy Popcorn. She hadn't liked the name Chucky wanted, and his dad had walked out of the room when Chucky said it. Chucky smiled, remembering. It was the first time he'd said the 'F' word out loud, and he'd made it rhyme with his own name. Better than Popcorn, he thought, even better than Poopcorn, which is what he whispered to the dog when he was able to get close to his quick little dog body.

Nancy poured Chardonay into the wine glasses. Laughter floated in from the living room. She heard Betty Clark say, "Remember last time we were here? Chucky locked himself in the powder room and flooded it?" Nancy's fingers sought the anchor pin. She prayed today wasn't going to turn into a Chucky roast.

Later, over a nearly empty lunch plate, she was able to relax. The chicken dish was a success, the salad, praised. In the center of the table the flowers nodded heavy heads.

Blood red cranberry juice dripped leisurely off the edge of the lunch table into a growing pool on the floor below. Chucky settled a sneaker in the middle of it and watched the new direction the puddle took.

"Chucky, the other children are going out for recess." Laurie sat down across from him. "You'll have to go to the time out room. Remember, no recess when you touch the children in inappropriate ways."

"This juice is sticky," he whispered.

"You need to look at me, Chucky, and speak so I can hear you. Go along to Time Out now."

"His mother's going to be freaking furious, if he doesn't earn cooking today." Noreen, Laurie's aide, announced this with authority. "The more time he spends away from home, the happier that woman is."

"Go on, Chucky, to Time Out," Laurie urged.

Chucky clumped into the coatroom, which served as Time Out and sat down heavily on a too-small chair. Did Noreen think he couldn't hear? He could hear just fine, but she talked about him as if he was a deaf boy, a lump. That's what Mrs. Karas, his teacher last year, called him.

"He's such a lump," she said one morning, sitting at her desk and drinking coffee.

A lump of what? Chucky wondered. A lump of Play Doh? A lump of dirt? A lump of dog poop? He smiled and rocked the chair. Mrs. Karas was the lump. Mrs. Karas sitting at her desk all day, yelling at kids.

"Did I see you get out of your seat?" she'd scream at him, and his breath would disappear. "Look at me when I talk to you." Turning to Noreen, she'd ask, "Can you explain something? Can you tell me why he looks everywhere but at me when I talk to him? What is wrong with him?"

He smiled. He wasn't sorry he'd peed on Mrs. Karas's fur coat. He could control his pee.

After the others returned from recess, Laurie lined everyone up, and Noreen marched them to the library in the basement. There they bumped into each other as they moved around, because the library shelves were crowded into one end of Mr. Mack's science room. Chucky stood stroking several books before picking one to open. Words everywhere, pages and pages of words. He closed the book and took the one next to it. Here, along with words, were drawings of cars and boats and planes, drawings of all the different parts of them, their insides and their outsides. He brought one of the drawings up close to his eyes.

"Great pictures, aren't they, Chuck?" Mr. Mack's voice made him jump. The book fell from his grasp, but Mr. Mack caught it. "I especially like the top views, see, here on page twenty-five." He thumbed through the book, then held it out for Chucky to see. "And did you notice this?" He fumbled for a minute with a page before opening it to reveal a double-page of a brightly colored sailboat. He folded the picture back into place and put the book into Chucky's hands.

11

Chucky's fingers gripped the book's hard covers. He listened to Mr. Mack's footsteps recede. Clutching the book to his stomach, he approached the table where Noreen sat, signing out the children's books.

"I don't have all day, Mr. Christmas. Let's see that book." She frowned at the title. "What's this? You can't read this, it's a junior high book." She dropped it into the box behind her. "Move, Chucky! Go get a picture book and hurry up about it."

Chucky stood still. He watched Amanda's sneakers begin a jumpy dance.

Noreen sighed as she came around the table. Grabbing Chucky by the arm, she trotted him along beside her to the nearest shelf. "Here," she said, pushing a large, flat book toward him. "You like dogs." She removed a card from the back page and, leaning on the table, wrote hastily on it.

"All right, kids," she called. "Line up, let's go." She led them to the steps to the main floor.

"Noreen!" Rita's horrified call kicked waves of excitement through the damp basement hallway. "Look! Look what Chucky's doing with the book you gave him!"

The sound of women's chatter hung over the card tables in the Christmas's living room, smothering any spark of commitment to the bridge games at hand. Nancy heard her daughters in the kitchen.

"Here are your little girls," one of the women said.

The girls stood smiling, balancing back packs and after-school snacks, shyly greeting their mother's guests.

"Mama, Mrs. Klein said you should take my temp'ature. She thinks I'm getting a cold."

"Maybe it's your rosy cheeks, sweetie, they're a little chapped." Nancy felt her younger daughter's forehead. "You feel nice and cool, but play indoors, just to be on the safe side."

The girls pattered up the stairs as the phone began to ring. Nancy excused herself and took it in the kitchen. She listened, then cried, "But what has he done? He's been looking forward to cooking all week." She barely listened to the explanation. "Yes, but . . . I have a child here in need of my attention." Again she listened. "All right. I'll be there . . . as soon as I can get away."

After putting the phone down, Nancy stood for a moment in the quiet kitchen. In the sink the bubbles of detergent foam that crowned stacks of lunch plates and teetering coffee cups broke with soft hissing sounds. The dog wheezed in his basket, his curly gray sides rising and falling. A burst of laughter came from the living room.

"Nancy," one of the women called, "is everything all right?"

Chucky stood at the glass entrance door and watched the traffic on the street in front of the church hall. From down the hall came the chatter of the children in the kitchen, their voices pitched high. Outside a man and boy walked past, the man's hand on the boy's shoulder. His mother appeared, blocking his view. She pushed the door open, causing him to bumble backwards. Under her glare his eyes filled with tears and his lower lip lost its mooring.

"Don't you start," she said, teeth clenched. "Get in the car. I'll tell Laurie we're leaving."

The ride home was uninterrupted by conversation. Chucky sat in the back seat and picked at the upholstery. He wondered if his father would be home for dinner.

"You're starting to irritate me." That was his father's warning bell, which he shook at all of them. The house filled with its peals.

"Well, we're home," Nancy announced, bringing the car to an abrupt stop in the driveway. Undoing her seatbelt, she swiveled in order to look at him and slapped the car keys against the seat back. "I hope you're happy, Chucky. You've managed to ruin my bridge club two years in a row. The only social life I have. Other than those invitations to meet with the mothers of your classmates. So I can talk about the problems of raising a special child. Some special, Chucky!" Her voice had climbed up into her forehead. "Well, no thanks. Anyhow, you understand what's going on. You and I know that. So I hope you're pleased with yourself, Chucky, real pleased." With a push she left the car, closing the door with a firm bam.

In the back seat darkness Chucky rocked and smiled. "I'm real pleased with myself." It came out a whisper. He wasn't in charge of his voice.

The End

GRIEF

T HE LEAVES were a problem. Murphy found himself worrying about them before he got out of bed in the morning. Some days he didn't bother with breakfast. Armed with a rake, and with the tentative fingers of early light working themselves between the houses, he pushed open the back screen door, his face a map of frown lines, and went out to do battle. He took it personally, all those leaves. Most weren't even his but swept down the hill and stubbornly settled on his walk and covered the small square of his front yard.

Had he noticed them in past years? He couldn't remember. Oh, he'd raked them all right, but had there been this many? He didn't think so.

After they were in piles, he bagged them, a job in itself. Once that was finally done, he got the broom and dustpan and swept up the bits and pieces and the dust, and that would do it. Until the next morning or, as autumn deepened and they came down like rain, until afternoon. Then, with the shadows creating pyramids of the rooftops on the houses across the street, he'd go back out, stroke after angry stroke of the rake fighting the onslaught.

One thing he could say for the raking, it left him worn out, so, while his legs often trembled and his hands shook as he fixed himself a bowl of soup or an egg for supper, at least he was able to sleep. Get comfortable in his chair to watch the news and next thing he knew, it was past eleven and he'd go upstairs and fall into bed. Sleep all night.

The summer had been different. Sometimes he had lain awake for hours, the house so quiet, even in the daytime, that it would fill his ears like the worst kind of noise. It hadn't bothered him when Rose was in the hospital, or even those months when she was in the nursing home. He'd been busy then, keeping things up against her return.

The locust leaves were the worst, clinging to the grass and sidewalk, thin and hard to get at. Reminded him of Colleen. He thought of her now as he worked the bristles of the broom between the cracks in the sidewalk. Rose had had a hard delivery, and it turned out Colleen was the only baby they could have. Stubborn as a locust leaf she'd been since day one. Every Friday she came, ever since the funeral, no matter that he'd told her not to bother, that he was getting along fine. She thought he needed constant looking after. Leaving dishes of food in the refrigerator, picking up discarded newspapers, changing the sheets on his bed. He could do those things if he had a mind to.

He scooted the dog aside with a wave of the broom. The dog had shown up mid-summer, thin as a rail and eager to please. Murphy had always fancied having a dog, but Rose hadn't wanted the mess. "Think of the fleas and the shedding," she'd declared whenever he brought up the subject. So he'd gone without. After all, it was Rose who had the care of the house. At first he'd allowed the dog inside, but she'd pissed on the rug, so Murphy had fixed her a bed in a corner of the porch, where she was sheltered from the worst of the wind and rain.

Whistling to the dog, Murphy gathered the rake and broom. He deliberately kept his eyes away from the house next door, knowing that Alma Mossman would be at her afternoon post in the front window. He'd made the mistake of returning her wave one day, and she'd been on him in a flash. "Come in and have a cup of tea, Tom," she'd called, and he'd had a hell of a time getting out of it. What she was up to, he didn't know, watching his every move, but he wasn't going to start being neighborly with widows, that was for darn sure.

It was the next day that Murphy had to chase off the dog. When he went out on the front stoop to get the paper, he saw her tearing into the bags—leaves flying everywhere, tossed into the air with each swing of her head. Her short little legs were splayed, her head close to the ground and moving in purposeful arcs, back and forth amid showers of leaves. It took him nearly an hour to clean up the mess she'd made. Afterwards, he went out back, closed the gate, and removed her bed. The cardboard carton, the old porch swing pillow and frayed blanket he'd found at the bottom of a basket in the basement laundry—he thrust all of them into one of the plastic leaf bags and put the bag next to the garbage can at the side of the house.

He didn't sleep well that night. Indigestion. It used to worry him that his heart was acting up, the pain sharp and right there deep in his chest. At Rose's urging he'd finally gone to the doctor. The doctor had done a lot of tests—too many, as far as Murphy was concerned—and told him to cut back on coffee and spicy foods and drink a glass of warm water when the pain occurred.

It was raining in the morning, one of those drenching autumn rains that darkened whole days. After rinsing out his oatmeal bowl and leaving the pot to soak, Murphy stood awhile in the front window and looked through the rain running down the glass like tears down cheeks. His bags of leaves lay at the curb, surrounded and covered over with the night's fresh fall.

Colleen came in mid-morning, dripping wet and juggling purse, keys, and what seemed like a dozen different bags of "father-aid," which was what Murphy called the food, clean laundry, reading material, and various household items she carted in every week. He did his usual grumbling, she her usual nagging, so that by the time she kissed his cheek and backed out the door, each was loaded up with enough guilt to last until her next visit.

He spent the afternoon dozing off and on in his recliner with the television droning and flickering across the room. He awoke with a start, suffering a moment or two of confusion. His first thought was Rose had forgotten to turn on the lamps. Then he remembered.

"Why?" The cry escaped him before he could clamp his lips on it, and it hung in the empty room.

THE END

GET USED TO IT

S HE WAS caught in traffic in the Lincoln Tunnel when she felt it. There beneath her left breast. A ripping sensation. She wasn't cold and clammy, wasn't nauseous, no pain down her left arm, just the feeling—something was tearing loose within her chest!

Sara's fear of tunnels and bridges registered one notch below her love of Broadway, so while it didn't rule out trips from Jersey to Manhattan, it did make them occasions when she needed to be hyper-alert. Later, when she was able to get her thoughts together and consider the heart thing calmly, it made sense that it would begin in a tunnel. What she did next was neither calm nor reasonable; she laid on the horn and flicked on the hazard lights. A security man, so furious that his eyes showed white around the irises, finally reached her car and found her bent over the steering wheel, her cheek pressed against it.

"My heart," she gasped, her voice barely audible in the cacophony the horn and its echoes created. "Oh, please . . . get me out of here."

"Whoa! And he did? Right out of the Lincoln Tunnel? In rush hour?" Billy, her youngest, rocked back in his chair, nearly spilling his coffee, as they sat around the old maple table in the kitchen late that night, the overhead light making cruel tracks in the lines of her face. All of them—two grown children and her sister—gaped at her, unfortunately, more impressed by her quick and dramatic exit from the tunnel than with the enormity of her rapidly deteriorating physical state.

Because, as she had tried to make the nurses and doctors understand at St. Clare's emergency room, where she was seen with surprising dispatch, her heart was tearing loose from its moorings. Dear God, she thought, no one understands—not my family, not the medical people. Her blood work and EKG had been normal the doctor announced in flawless, if stilted, English. "It is desirable you see your family doctor in the morning, if symptoms persist," he'd said. "But, Missus, I assure you. No signs of heart malfunction are present. You are, perhaps . . . overly wrought."

"Overly wrought," well, yes, that was true, she thought, and who wouldn't be? Hadn't her husband of nearly forty years left her to go to some God forsaken island half way around the world where he intended to build a water line for a bunch of unwashed natives? Never mind that he was an English professor with zero training in engineering. And her divorced sister, instead of being a source of empathy, kept telling her how she had to get used to being alone, as if it were some sort of desirable state. Didn't her cat have cancer and weren't her sons refusing to speak to one another? Hadn't her daughter announced she was a lesbian? So anyone with a brain in his or her head could see she had good cause to be . . . what? Crazy? A lunatic? Yes, she thought, a lunatic, but one whose <u>heart</u> was coming undone!

"Here, Mom." Sam put a plate of ravioli in front of her. "You should eat," her daughter said, adding a chunk of garlic bread to the plate. Her heavy watchband made a metallic clang against the china.

"I have to be true to my own sexuality," Sam had announced, standing in the middle of the bedroom a week after her father had left for Indonesia. "Dad's shown me the way. He was brave enough to say, 'The hell with this barren, stifling, middle class life. I'm off to help the less fortunate.'" She'd thrust her hands into the pockets of her slacks, her legs spread in a fighter's stance, and continued, "Well, I'm declaring my independence from the do-what's-expected-of-you life. I love Amelia. We're going to make a life together, and you'll just have to get used to it."

Sara had looked at her, her only daughter, in her stiff white shirt, gabardine pants suit, and thick brown oxfords, hair in a short, near-buzz cut—all that was lacking was a tie—and she'd wanted to wring her goddamn neck. She'd also wanted to remind her that it was that "barren, stifling, middle class life" that had bought her four years at a first-rate university and two years of law school. Her daughter wasn't big on gratitude.

"And after you eat, you need to get some sleep," Sam said. "I'm sure Dr. Christy will be able to find out what's wrong with you. I'll call him first thing tomorrow morning."

Which she did. If there was one thing Sam was good at, it was getting what she wanted. To a nurse's, "Every appointment's filled. We have something open three weeks from Tuesday," she herself would quail where Sam charged ahead and got an immediate appointment.

Immaculate in his white coat, Dr. Christy sat in the examining room on the edge of a padded stool and raised a skeptical eyebrow toward his neatly combed gray hair. His silver-framed glasses reflected the light, making his eyes inaccessible, but the thin, questioning eyebrow said it all.

She felt desperation well up past her loose heart into her throat. "But I don't care what the X-Rays and the EKG say. I felt it again this morning, this . . . this feeling that something's ripping inside me. It's got to be my heart—it's right where a heart should be," she cried, placing her hand over her left breast. "Right here!"

Without a word he rose and for a second time slid the cold, round end of his stethoscope under the paper gown she'd donned for the examination, his eyes fixed on the opposite wall as he concentrated on the heartbeats it communicated to his ears.

"Perfectly normal," he pronounced, sitting back down on the stool's edge. "I can order an ECHO. That way you'll be able to see for yourself." And here he allowed the hint of a small, patronizing smile tug at his pale lips. "You'll like the test . . . noninvasive, and you can actually see the heart and its vessels . . . all in their proper places, I'm sure." He rose, patting her knee. "Stress does strange things, my dear, strange things."

After she dressed and made an appointment to have the ECHO cardiogram later in the week, she wandered into the street. What to do? What to do? she asked herself, watching noon time traffic creep by. Here she was, a woman who would soon have a free-floating heart—oh! There it went again! And no one believed her.

The rector lived alone in the large, gloomy manse behind St. Luke's. On the front porch she hesitated after lifting the cherubim-shaped brass knocker, thinking that perhaps she should wait and see him in his office at the church. But surely even on his day off he'd see a parishioner in distress. She let the knocker drop, then rapped it a few extra times, because Herbert—she refused to call him 'Father'—was, despite his protestations, losing his hearing.

She waited, trying to concentrate on the emerging blossoms on the dogwood that tossed in the spring wind, breathing in shallow little gasps so as not to cause further damage in her chest. After another series of good, strong raps of the knocker failed to rouse him, she left the porch and made her way on an uneven brick path to the rear of the house. There, through the glass in the door she saw him at the kitchen table where he appeared to be doing something with a rolling pin. She tapped on the glass, startling him. He turned, mystified for a moment before a look of recognition cleared his features, and he shuffled to the door in scuffed bedroom slippers that were having trouble staying on his feet.

"My, my," he murmured, "you gave me quite a scare. Come in—don't mind the mess—I'm making cookies, you see."

Herbert had been the priest at St. Luke's Episcopal for as long as she could remember. A kindly man, he'd slipped easily into senior citizen status along with much of his dwindling congregation. He'd been a widower for a number of years, and she hoped that might give him insight into her situation, both of them having been left alone.

"Cookies? Whyever for, Herb?" The table was a disaster field of flour, balls of crumbled dough, baking tins, and cookie cutters worn thin with age.

He attempted to brush flour from the front of his shirt, which had escaped his pants. "The grandchildren," he explained. Peering more closely at her, he asked, "Is everything all right?"

In his study they sat close to the fireplace where a gas jet burned cheerfully, she in an enveloping wing chair, he in an ancient caned rocker, mugs of tea that he had insisted on brewing, close at hand. And she recounted her story to the accompaniment of his comforting umm's and I see's. If nothing else, Herb was an attentive listener, perhaps because of his faulty hearing, and her hopes rose as his attention gathered her in.

"So you see how desperately I need help . . . surgery—or maybe one of those wires threaded through my arteries—<u>something</u>!"

"Umm . . . yes . . . yes, something is needed, I see that." He continued to rock, and the creaking wood and the ticking of the clock on the wall soothed her.

"The altar guild needs volunteers," he said.

She was afraid she'd misunderstood him. "What?" she asked. "The altar guild?"

"Just the thing, I believe. The quiet of the sacristy . . . being in the proximity of the altar . . . very healing, very healing indeed."

She stopped for a container of coffee at the bakery, choosing three pieces of rugelach to eat with it. Carrying them to the car, she wondered if they would constitute her last meal. The heaviness in her chest was becoming unbearable, and leaving the rectory, she had decided to return home to die in her own bed, a better choice, she was convinced, than a hospital room.

Turning onto Stelfox, she silently blessed the town for repaving it, sparing her fragile chest the bumps and jars of the potholes of winter. Inside the house, she stood a moment, catching her breath, missing the usual greeting from Chester, a cat who had once relished heights, now prevented by his cancer from moving freely about. The tumor on his leg was outpacing her ability to accept it and the future it held for both of them. Shedding her coat on the floor to avoid raising her arms to hang it in the closet, she found Chester in his basket under the kitchen table.

"Oh, sweetie," she cried, for the tumor was oozing pus and blood. She gingerly lowered herself onto a chair and gently gathered up the confused creature in the blanket he lay on, and carried him upstairs. They were nestled under a voluminous comforter with the empty coffee container and crumbs from the rugelach on the bedside table, when she heard the front door bang open. A few minutes later, Billy came clumping in.

"Still got that pain, huh?" he asked, making room for himself on the side of the bed.

"You'll have to get your own dinner," she whispered and was relating instructions on how he should go about this when she saw that he was staring at the comforter.

"Jeezus! You're bleeding!" he cried, leaping to his feet as he pointed to a swath of blood.

"No, no, not me—it's Chester," she explained.

Billy uncovered Chester, his face curling into horror at the sight of the cat's leg, grotesque in shape, leaking gore.

"Oh, my God—what a mess! You got to get him to Nate."

Nate, her older son, was a vet. "You'll have to do it," she said. "I can't . . . my heart . . ."

He ran an anxious hand over his face. "How can I?" he whined. "You know we're not speaking."

"Well, you'll have to," she said, surprised at the firmness of her voice. "Anyhow, I'm sick of listening to the two of you. It's high time you hashed things out between yourselves. You're adults, for God's sake." She hiked herself up to a sitting position, hugging Chester to her aching chest. "Poor baby," she murmured into the fur of his neck. "I love you."

She eased him toward Billy. "Take him to your brother," she commanded through her tears. Pointing toward the door, she cried, "Now go!"

She remained upright after hearing the front door close and the roar of Billy's Mustang rise from the driveway. Facing her husband's chest of drawers across the room, she stared at the neat pile of his black, calf-high socks from Brooks Brothers, lying on top. He'd decided he wouldn't need socks in Indonesia. "I know it won't tear your heart out to see me go," he'd said, standing in front of the bureau as he announced his intended departure.

THE END

THE SAMARITAN

S HE SAW the man as she entered the tunnel, which wasn't a real tunnel, but a dark, verdant passage of the road running through a mile-long length of woods. It was unusual to see pedestrians along that stretch, especially one dressed for business. Wearing a dark gray suit, he was walking with traffic and, from the length of his stride appeared young, although his shoulders were hunched, perhaps from fatigue. That was her first thought; her reaction was one that she never understood.

"Care for a lift?"

He didn't hesitate for a moment, but grasped the handle, swung the car door wide, and slid quickly onto the passenger seat. The odor of dust and oil accompanied him, and she saw that, up close, he wasn't as reputable looking as she'd thought. The white shirt that accompanied the gray suit was limp with age, the seams yellowish, the neck frayed.

Steering back onto the road, she darted glances at him—a striped necktie, askew and so thin it looked one-dimensional, above it his face, the jaw line firm but in need of a shave, skin the color of oatmeal.

"I'm going as far as Edgemont," she said, naming the next town. "Will that help?"

He nodded, staring straight ahead.

"Miss your bus? So easy to do. Their schedules are erratic at best . . . don't you think? And for what they charge in fares . . ." She was chattering; probably nerves.

Never, ever pick up a hitchhiker, even a woman: her husband's words, first uttered way back before they were married and often repeated. It was actually one of his rules. He had so many that it was easy to overlook one, she rationalized. Still, she'd never broken the hitchhiker one. Until today.

But, God, the August heat, the air moist and heavy, the temperature in the high eighties even though it was only a little after nine in the morning. Even walking in the shade would do one in, especially dressed in a wool suit with a shirt and tie. Surely her husband would understand.

She slowed for the blinking yellow at the intersection that brought them out of the tunnel. "I'll pull over by the Chinese restaurant, if that's okay. Then you'll just need to cross the street for the New York bus."

But he was asleep! Or—oh, Lord—passed out? Jerking the wheel hard to the right, she barely missed getting clipped from behind, a horn making an arc of angry protest as the offended car gunned past them.

She threw her car into park and swung to face him. His head rested on the support, mouth slightly open, eyes closed, but his chest was moving, and she could hear the soft hiss of air with each escaping exhale. "Oh, thank God," she gasped. "Sir?" Poking his shoulder lightly, she whispered, "Sir . . . are you okay?"

With eyelids fighting to open and stay that way, he mumbled something. It sounded like "hungry."

"You're hungry?"

With some effort—she could see the cords in his neck tighten—he raised his head from the support and rocked forward in the seat.

She put out a hand to steady him, feeling heat and the surprising thinness of his upper arm through the rough cloth. "Have you eaten?" she asked. "Did you eat breakfast?"

He stared ahead for what seemed to her the longest time before shaking his head. Shifting his eyes, which were an opaque blue and rimmed in pink, he met her gaze. "No," he said softly. Looking away, he said it again, louder the second time.

Her mind was skating on the thin ice of possibilities. She was on her way to, not from, the market, so she had no food in the car. Perhaps one of the children's candy bars in the glove compartment? But, no, if any were there, they'd be an inedible mass of chocolate in the heat of summer days. A glance at the restaurant's dark interior confirmed it was closed, and the supermarket was several miles further up the road. But the Edgemont Diner, only a block away, would be open. Just the thing!

Parking was in the rear. When she urged him to leave the car, he sat limp and unmoving, looking not at her but through the windshield at the wall that skirted the lot.

"I'll get you something," she told him, clearing her throat to keep her voice from cracking. But when asked what he'd like, she was met with a weak shake of his head. Leaving the air conditioning on, she left him.

Inside the diner, in the bright light and din of voices and background music, she leaned against a wall to slow her breathing and rein in her thinking. She had screwed up by offering the ride, no argument there, leaving her to deal with a sick man. Her husband would kill her, an event that would nevertheless have to wait while she figured out what to do. First, food, she decided. After that, she'd . . . call the police? An ambulance? She'd see.

Standing by the cash register, waiting for the egg sandwich she had ordered, she worked a napkin from the chrome holder. Her other hand, idly resting in her skirt pocket, suddenly tensed. A frantic search of the pocket came up with no car key. As quickly as the heat, which flooded her and caused her knees to weaken, rose, it dissipated as she recalled leaving the car running for the air conditioning. And, of course, she thought, the car! It was the car he wanted.

Outside she skidded around the corner of the diner . . . and saw it, parked where she'd left it, the sun bouncing off the rear window. As she approached, she dabbed at her eyes, tearing in the light, with the napkin she still clutched.

He was gone. The key was in the ignition, although he'd switched the engine off. The glove box gaped open, and if there'd been candy bars there, they were gone. A quick check revealed that both insurance and registration papers were where they belonged in a plastic sleeve. Nothing was missing.

On her way home, driving through the tunnel, she saw that her hands still shook. She kept her eyes on the road, silently praying she wouldn't see him. There was no need to mention the incident to her husband, she'd decided. The man had simply been a pedestrian in need . . . and she had come to his aid.

THE END

THE KOREAN

C OMMERCE IN the town of Aspinhill, New Jersey, consisted of a bank, a pizza parlor, a florist shop, a deli, and a dentist's office. That was the extent of the business district. Emily Craig worked in the dental office, within walking distance of her home on Stelfox Street.

During her lunch hour on a windy day in early March, she crossed the street to Borough Hall and climbed the steps to the planning board office, where she located Helen Colby, the secretary, behind a desk strewn with architectural renderings, engineers' specifications, and blue prints.

"Afternoon, Emily," Helen greeted her. "Come to see the plans for number thirteen? Whole neighborhood's been flocking in." She placed an array of papers on the counter.

Emily looked down at the top sheet. On it was a line drawing of a large, brick house. "What's this, Helen?"

"That's it, Emily. That's what he plans to build."

"He?"

"Mr. Kim. You know, the man who bought the house across from yours when old Tom Rieders died."

"Helen," Emily said patiently, "there's already a house there, and it's certainly not this . . . this huge thing." She jabbed a finger at the paper.

Helen shrugged her sparse, sandy eyebrows. "Right. This is the house he plans to build once the present house is razed."

"Razed? What—knocked down? He's going to knock down a beautiful little house and build <u>that</u>?" Her right index finger danced on the drawing, her voice sounding as though it were coming out of her forehead. "Can he <u>do</u> that? Knock over a perfectly good house?"

"He owns it," Helen said. "There's a planning board meeting about it next Tuesday. Better come early, there's not a lot of chairs in the room where they meet."

The planning meeting to consider the requested variances for thirteen Stelfox was not a happy affair. The turn-out was large and the tenor of the night was anger. One by one, householders set forth their objections. Square footage, the removal of an old maple and an even older oak, the new house's very presence, all were contested. Late in the evening, a well-dressed Asian man hesitantly approached the microphone and, facing the crowd, introduced himself as Donald Kim. His eyes were wells of liquid brown sadness. Emily lowered her own to avoid seeing the tears she was certain were about to weep down his cheeks.

"I . . . want . . . build . . . beautiful house . . . for you." The sincerity of his words introduced guilt into the room, and the response was an uncomfortable silence. Taking advantage of the stillness, the chairman hastily ended the meeting.

"What did you think of the 'beautiful house' speech?" David Craig asked Emily in the car on the way home.

"It's not a beautiful house is what I think. It's too big, it has no character, and I don't believe building a beautiful house for the residents of Stelfox Street is his top priority."

"Problem is, if the board turns him down on this one, he'll get a different set of plans. Sooner or later, we'll get his beautiful house."

David proved to be right. Although variances were denied for the first house, a third set of plans was approved. The new house, which one of the neighbors called a faux Tudor, held its sides in and fit, albeit snugly, between the contested maple and oak trees.

"Damn!" Emily exploded, when she heard of the board's decision.

"It's only a house, Emily."

"Oh, David, right across the street, practically in my garden."

"You're the one who's always telling me change is what life is all about. Well, welcome to change."

The following Monday Mr. Kim arrived in front of number thirteen at seven a.m. and, as a general the day before battle, began to amass and ready his forces. Wires were detached, gas and water pipes capped, and several small trees removed. The high point was the off-loading of a yellow backhoe from a flatbed truck.

Emily, who didn't work on Mondays, watched the array of workers and vehicles to a tune of growing agitation. "I had planned on planting phlox," she told David that evening, "but I retreated in the face of Mr. Kim's onslaught. At least I'll be at work the rest of the week and won't have to witness the house coming down."

The house was leveled in one day. "Just a couple of hours, and it was a pile of rubble," Eliot Gould told her.

"David, I've written a letter to the editors of the <u>Northern Valley News</u>. See what you think." She handed him a sheet of paper along with the day's mail.

". . . in a town already developed to capacity . . . ruining the make-up of a long-established neighborhood . . ." He looked up. "I hope Mr. Kim doesn't see this. Don't think he'll like the 'eyesore' reference."

"I hope he does see it. Maybe he'll get the message."

"Maybe we haven't considered <u>his</u> message."

As the house rose, the work force changed often, but Mr. Kim was a constant. In the late afternoons, after the workers drove their rusting vans down the street under the heavy, dusty foliage of summer, he moved over the lot, picking up empty coffee containers and stray plastic bags; stacking scattered boards into neat piles; checking the day's work close up. Only then did he climb into his car and drive away.

The house rose: concrete blocks formed the foundation; uprights were followed by plywood, bricks, and siding; the sound of hammers, saws, and drills wounded the summer air.

By autumn work on the house had neared completion. Emily moved through the garden in the cool, late October sunshine, systematically burying fat daffodil bulbs. Although it was Sunday, Mr. Kim's car and a red van were parked in the wide new driveway at number thirteen. Emily tried to concentrate on the bulb-planting ritual, but she wasn't feeling the peace that usually attended it.

"He knows he's not allowed to work on Sundays," she exclaimed to David.

David glanced up from the Sunday <u>Times</u>.

"I called the building inspector the first time they worked over there on a Sunday." At the sight of David's raised eyebrows, she protested, "The neighborhood deserves one day a week of peace and quiet. And there is a statute forbidding Sunday construction."

David just looked at her for a long moment, then said, "Have a cup of tea, Em. Mr. Kim is in a hurry to sell—and he knows the market is falling."

She took a deep breath. "I suppose I should look at it this way: the sooner he finishes, the sooner he'll move on to another unsuspecting neighborhood. But . . . I'm hoping he won't be able to sell. Serve him right!' She slammed the door behind her.

The sky sulked overhead as Emily swung an ax at the prone Christmas tree, removing its branches. These she arranged throughout the garden, graceful arms stretched over perennials and buried bulbs, protecting them from the thaws and icings of winter.

"Ready for snow, Emily?" Varina Gould stopped by the garden wall.

"I think so, Varina." She set the ax down carefully.

"Smells like snow. Hope our friend has a snow shovel." They looked across at number thirteen. Just then the outside lights went on. "He comes and turns those lights on in the afternoon, then comes back in the morning to turn them off. Have you noticed? You have to admit, he takes good care of it."

"He should, it's a million dollar investment."

"I can't imagine who's going to pay that much for such a small piece of property. Well, I'll let you finish, Emily, see you later."

Standing at the front window four months later, Emily said, "April fool!"

"Who's the April fool?" David asked, joining her.

She nodded at Mr. Kim, sitting in his car in the driveway across the street. "What if the house <u>never</u> sells?"

"He missed the sellers' market by a couple of months. I suppose the bank that financed it will foreclose on him."

Emily pulled the curtain aside. "Sometimes he sits in his car for hours, looking at the darn place—or, as he would say, the beautiful house he built for us. He's a lonely figure, isn't he?"

Wind-thrashed day lilies slapped at Emily's legs. She pulled the slicker hood over her head as she hurried to the front door. It's far from that proverbial rare day in June, she thought. The oak tree across the street groaned, threatening Mr. Kim's car with its flailing branches.

"Have we ever had such a cold, gloomy, wet, awful spring?" she asked David at dinner that evening. "And you know, David, Mr. Kim's car has been over there since I got home late this afternoon, but the lights on the house aren't on."

In the early hours of the following morning, Emily woke to a light show playing on the bedroom ceiling. She shook David.

He pushed his way to a sitting position. "What?" he muttered. "What's going on?" He fought the covers, finally making his way out of bed and across the room to the windows.

"Police . . . across the street," he muttered.

Emily joined him. They watched as another police car swept up to brake sharply in front of their own house. Lights flashed eerily through the diamond-paned windows of the new house, as policemen moved through empty rooms.

David pulled on an old sweatshirt and pants. Emily watched him emerge from the front door below and join Eliot Gould, who had just arrived from up the street.

Steady light now flowed from the house. An ambulance backed into the driveway and parked beside Mr. Kim's car. She saw David go over to one of the policemen. He was telling David something, his arms and hands eloquent in their swoops and soundlessness, as he pointed toward the house. The front door banged and she heard David on the steps.

"What happened?" she cried.

He joined her at the window, slipping an arm around her shoulders, his wet raincoat between them.

"The police got a call from Kim's wife. She was upset, worried that he hadn't come home. They just found him. He's sick, Em. They're taking him to the Pines."

"Pines? The county hospital? What's wrong with him?" she managed to whisper.

"He's not making sense. Doesn't know where he is, who he is . . . police found him sitting on the floor."

They watched as the volunteer ambulance people bumped a gurney out of the front door of the new house. Bathed in the entrance light that the police had turned on, Emily could see they had Mr. Kim on it, his struggles to get free of a blanket and heavy cloth straps, fruitless.

August light bathed the garden. Emily paused to appreciate the warmth, the color, the heady fragrance. From inside she could hear David's contented whistle.

"How was church?" he asked.

"The Gospel lesson was the parable of the Good Samaritan." She pushed newspapers aside and sat beside him on the couch. "And the sermon was about our response to the parable's message." She was quiet for a moment. "I gave Varina a ride home. Know what she said as she got out of the car? She said, 'The new house looks kind of nice, doesn't it, Emily?'" She started for the stairs. "And then she told me that she heard it was sold."

THE END

A DAY IN THE COUNTRY

H EAT IS rolling through summer like a Sherman tank. Edward and I are in our first home, an old Arts and Craft cottage with wonderful iron radiators but no central air conditioning. This morning when the phone rings, it's Edward, who, I should note, is in his 72 degree office. "What's for dinner?" he asks. When you aren't panting and covered with perspiration, you can think about food.

"Barbecued chicken—from the supermarket."

"Oh. Okay. Hey, guess who called me? Danny."

"Your brother Danny?"

"Yes, my brother Danny. Do we know any other Danny?"

"Guess not." I hesitate. "How is he?"

"The same. Well . . . actually, he was upset. Something with his boss."

"Nothing new there. He always has trouble with bosses."

". . . I asked him out for the weekend."

"Here? This weekend?"

"Yeah, well. Anyway, it'll be more like twenty-four hours. I mean, is it a problem, asking my own brother?"

"No . . . only . . ."

"Only?"

"Only the last time you talked to your own brother, you hung up on him and swore you'd never speak to him again. He was, to use your words, 'a stupid, sniveling, conniving excuse of a human being.' Only that."

"Oh, yeah. Well, he said something about how a day in the country would be . . . 'healing,' I think he called it."

I sighed . . . silently. Danny thinks anything north of forty-second Street is the country.

That night, over macaroni salad and chicken, I say to Edward, "Both of us will need to make your brother feel welcome." I pause, but he says nothing. "You know, not lose our tempers . . . or get nasty." He's looking across the chicken carcass at me, a considering kind of expression on his face. I pretend not to notice and chase an errant macaroni on my plate.

"<u>Our</u> tempers? You mean <u>my</u> temper. It's okay, you can say it. You don't lose your temper with my brother."

"No, that's not true. I'm as guilty as you. He can be extremely exasperating. But you did invite him to our home, and we should be gracious hosts. And patient, because he's never going to change—no matter how many lessons you teach him."

"Okay, you're right. Be mature. Act like an adult. I can do that."

I push home my point. "Yes, you can. And after he leaves, we'll compare notes. First one to speak rudely loses."

"What?"

"What do you mean, what?"

"What do we lose?" He runs a chicken bone through his teeth and drops it onto his plate.

"I didn't mean it literally."

"No, I like it. We'll have an incentive." He wipes his mouth and then each finger with his napkin. "What are the stakes?"

"No stakes." I push back my chair. "You know I don't bet."

He shrugs. "Really? Well, then . . ."

"Okay," I say quickly. "We'll have an incentive—a <u>small</u> incentive. How about the winner . . . doesn't have to empty the dishwasher for a week?"

He waves his hand impatiently. "Uh-uh. Too small. We need something with a bigger payoff." His brow furrows. "Okay, here it is: the winner gets to choose the wallpaper for the hall—with no interference from the loser. What do you think?" A sly grin spreads across his face. He knows my weaknesses.

"It's tempting."

"All right! We've got a deal."

The pattern for the new wallpaper has been a bone of contention for months. It's mutually agreed that the old paper has to be replaced, but that's where mutuality ends. Edward wants something only Picasso would approve, I want what he calls 'blah.' Knowing Danny's ability to drive Edward over the edge, I see my chance.

When Danny calls from the local bus station on Saturday morning, Edward answers the phone, and a brief conversation ensues. Slamming down the receiver, Edward shouts, "<u>We're</u> goddamn <u>here</u>!"

"What? What are you talking about? And stop yelling."

"That's what my brother said! <u>We're</u> here! Now who the hell is <u>we</u>?"

"You didn't ask?"

"No, I didn't ask! Goddamn it, he's started already! That's it! The hell with him!" He throws his car keys on the hall table.

"Calm down. Are you sure he didn't say he'd be bringing someone? Think."

"<u>Think</u>? I don't have to <u>think</u>! He never said <u>anything</u> about bringing <u>anyone</u>!" Edward, for the most part, is a quiet man, but around his older brother . . . he yells a lot.

"This is getting us nowhere. You'll have to pick him—or them—up, so you'd better get started. I'll make up the other bed in the guest room."

"<u>Goddamn</u> <u>it</u>!"

"Go. And remember . . . be pleasant." I smile. Wallpaper patterns are dancing through my head.

He returns with Danny and a small, neatly put together woman. I vaguely recall Danny telling me about a woman he met at an AA meeting.

"Abbie! Abbie, my favorite sister-in-law! Abbie, my love!" Danny gives me a bear hug, introduces Marie, who seems pleasant, and we all carry tote bags and weekend cases into the house. Edward, looking like a poster boy for genial hosts, holds the door for everyone.

Marie seems a genuinely nice person, but, although attractive, she has a severe facial tic that commands my attention no matter how hard I try to ignore it. In addition, she tells us that she suffered a stroke in the worst days of her alcoholism and sustained damage to her speech. I'm sympathetic but notice nothing wrong until we're at lunch. Relating an incident that occurred on the bus ride from the city, she says, "All the seats were obsolete, so the man stood, and that made the driver all the muddier."

Edward and I, confused, stare at her, but Danny continues to serve himself more salad. "Occupied, Marie, made the driver madder." He looks thoughtful. "Actually that should be angrier."

I smile nervously and don't look in Edward's direction. After lunch he, Marie, and I leave the table and are on our way out of the dining room before we notice that Danny has remained seated.

"Abbie, how about a cup of coffee?" He taps his glass of untouched ice tea. "I can't drink this stuff."

"Oh, sorry. Sure, I'll make you coffee. Marie, how about you? Would you like coffee?"

"No, no. The ice tea was plasty."

"Plenty," Danny says, following me to the kitchen. He watches closely as I take down a can of coffee and begin to spoon it into a filter.

"You don't grind beans?"

"No grinder," I explain.

"Oh . . . well."

By dinnertime I'm casting suspicious glances at my husband, who's being unusually kind and patient with his brother. As I lift the filet of beef onto a serving dish, Danny wanders into the kitchen. "Looks good—if you eat meat."

The filet wobbles dangerously at the end of the fork.

"You don't eat <u>meat</u>?"

"No, didn't I tell you? I've become a vegetarian. Not a vegan, that may be in the future. But don't worry—and don't fuss. A little pasta will do just fine."

I cover the beef, put a lid on the dish of new potatoes, turn the fire off under the asparagus, shove the salad into the refrigerator, and grab a box of penne off the shelf.

After dinner, we linger at the table, drinking coffee and listening to another of Danny's stories. Finally, I slip into the kitchen and begin the clean-up, while he continues to hold forth. I come to the coffeepot on the warmer. "Danny, excuse me for interrupting, but do you or Marie want more coffee?"

Marie smiles and shakes her head. "None for me, or I won't dance."

"Sleep," Danny interprets as he considers my offer before covering his cup. "Nope. That's all for me."

"Sure? There's more here."

"J'ai fini."

Edward smiles benignly.

I pick up empty dessert plates and return to the kitchen. I'm putting the last dishes into the washer when I hear Danny call. "Abbie! Changed my mind. How about another cup of coffee? And some half and half, if you have it. You don't mind, do you?"

"But I did ask—"

"Yes?" Edward urges. "What did you ask, dear?"

"Nothing. Not important. I'll make a fresh pot." I think my hair's permanently plastered to the back of my neck, and beads of perspiration are rolling, one at a time, between my breasts. As I'm counting coffee measures, Danny calls again from the dining room. "What is it, Dan?" I ask, losing count.

"I said, 'Is it Colombian?' The coffee—is it Colombian coffee?"

I return to the dining room. "Colombian? I'm not sure. Do you want it, if—?"

Before I can finish, he turns to his brother and says, "Did I tell you that Marie and I discovered the best—let me repeat—the best Cuban restaurant in New York?"

"Danny?" I'm waiting, coffee can in hand.

"Is that so?" Edward asks. "What's it called?"

"The Cuban Cafe. Lines, there's always a line. You have to wait, minimum, forty-five minutes for a table. But the food is heavenly, and the . . ."

In the kitchen I scoop coffee into the filter. The hell with it. He asks, I'll swear it's grown, ground, and canned in goddamn Colombia!

At the table Danny is still singing the praises of the restaurant.

"Where is it, Dan?" Edward asks.

"In the Village. I know, I know, you rarely go south of 14th Street. Well, there's a lot of the city you're missing, my boy. So you'll have to put aside childish prejudices if you want to eat fantastic Cuban food. Right, Marie?"

Marie's eyes are glazed. She looks like someone composing the weekly shopping list. "Right," she agrees.

"Umm, Abbie, do I smell coffee?"

"Almost ready, Danny."

His fingers drum an expectant beat. "Want me to pour it?"

"It has another minute or two." I go out to the kitchen. The rich, steamy fragrance fills the air. The glass carafe glistens. I watch the fat drops plop from the filter. How soon before I can politely say "good night," I wonder? Not soon enough. I reach down a clean cup and saucer and pour the brewed coffee.

At the table Danny is elbow-deep in photo packets. "Look, dear." My husband is beaming like a proud parent. "Danny has pictures from his and Marie's weekend in Baltimore."

I set the coffee as close to Danny as the photos will allow. For the next hour we look at his pictures. I'm in awe of the thoroughness with which he's recorded a single weekend.

"This is our table at the dinner Saturday night . . . or was it Friday night? Marie?"

Pictures of backs of heads, of people I don't know, of every fish in the Baltimore aquarium. It's late . . . my eyes insist on closing.

Edward rises. "Marie, Dan, I love your pictures, but I must get my beauty sleep, so if you'll excuse me, I'll say 'good night.'" He kisses Marie and me and is gone before he can be roped into watching the late movie. I'm not as fortunate. But first, I carry Danny's coffee cup to the kitchen. It's full.

Sunday morning is hazy and hot. The window air conditioners are pausing, as in breaths not taken. Danny appears in bathing shorts. "A little country sun for this city boy," he announces. "Coffee, is there coffee, Abbie?"

"On the counter, Danny."

"It's not decaffeinated, is it?"

"Just drink the goddamn coffee!"

All eyes, wide with shock, swing to me. The kitchen is silent.

"Abbie?" Edward's eyebrows push into his hairline in a show of concern. "I apologize for her, Dan. Must be the heat." He pours his brother a mug of coffee. "Where did you say those wallpaper samples were, dear?"

At two-thirty, Danny is still upstairs. Marie, her bags packed and piled by the front door, is sitting with us in the family room, receiving approving glances from Edward, who is compulsively early, especially where transportation is involved. He begins to move about nervously, twitching the car keys in the palm of his hand. Finally, Danny appears, his skin a dangerous pink from his morning of sunbathing. Edward's smile is beginning to look stale. "We don't want to miss that three o'clock bus . . . do we?" The keys are twitching nonstop now.

The clock on the car dash reads 2:52 as we pull into the bus station. "I have to go to the bathroom," Danny announces.

"We just left the house ten minutes ago." Edward's voice is stretched tight. "Why the—why didn't you go back there?"

"I'll go over to the diner. Won't be but a sec."

We watch him saunter across the town square. Passing a young woman with a toddler, he stops, and we can see him pointing at the bus shelter and talking. The woman shakes her head and moves on. Danny continues to the diner.

"What's he doing?" Edward moans.

"Probably asking her what time the New York bus is due," I say.

"But we told him when it's due."

"I know."

He moans softly. We watch the road in silence.

"The bus!" he suddenly cries, reaching for the door handle. We scramble out of the car, pulling bags as we go.

"Here comes Danny!" I wave to him, stabbing my finger in the air toward the bus, which is lumbering to a stop. Handshakes, kisses, suitcases changing hands—I think Edward is about to cry.

Danny turns and leans toward us as gears grind and the doors begin to close. "See you for Christmas!" he shouts.

I look at my husband. The imminent tears have vanished. "Did you hear that?" he cries. "Did he say what I think he said?" Bus fumes swirl around us.

Threading my arm through his, I lead him to the car. "A lot can happen in four months. Maybe we'll move to Alaska. Danny hates cold weather."

"He said it, didn't he? He really thinks he's coming here for Christmas!"

"You won, Edward. You were a paragon of patience. Why, by Christmas the foyer and hallways will be covered with your choice of wallpaper."

He grins. "I did win, didn't I? You were ready to pour that coffee over his head." We get into the car and start home.

The End

THE PIANO TEACHER

S HE STANDS on the front doorstep, a plum-shaped woman of indeterminate age, her smile vague. She has come to teach piano to my stepdaughter, who, given to troubling spells of anxiety, surprised us by expressing an interest in learning to play. For over two years, dating to her mother's death, almost nothing had sparked her interest until this.

I invite the teacher in, careful to grasp tightly by his collar our Labrador, a sweet-tempered but curious dog whose attentions the woman tolerates in a manner that too closely smacks of martyrdom for me to admire. Once I've confined the dog to the kitchen and called to my stepdaughter, I attend to the pianist's needs. The use of the bathroom, she requests, and a glass of water, if that isn't too much trouble. She speaks softly, her voice a cobweb strand between us, demanding close attention for fear the connection will be lost.

My stepdaughter appears. Her hands—already tense—seek refuge, first in her skirt pockets, next clasped to her waist, but nothing suits, and they continue their vain journey. I encourage with a broad smile that doesn't do; she frowns, ducks her head, quickens her path to the piano bench.

I love my husband and have known from the time we first met that his daughter grieved deeply for her mother, whose death from pancreatic cancer had been sudden and dreadful, a five-week spiral from a life of baking brownies and running carpools to surgery and a fatal stroke. Time, that gentle healer, everyone agreed, would lessen the child's anguish and return her to the ordinary ups and downs of an eight year-old's life. Until then there were medication and a therapist, the latter reputed to have extraordinary success with childhood depression. The anguish did recede,

43

but its void was filled by an anxiety that rises and falls to an unrecognizable tune. I love my husband, but I worry that his daughter's dark angel will separate us with its black widespread wings.

The teacher returns with silent steps from the bathroom. I point out the glass of water I've set on the small table next to her customary chair near the piano and leave them, noticing as I turn to go the brightening of my stepdaughter's face as she and the woman exchange greetings. For the next forty-five minutes they will work together in harmony, the girl free of her personal nightmares and closer to joy than she'll come in the seven days until her next lesson.

In the laundry I finish folding clothes, the fabrics soft and smelling of the outdoors even though they come straight from the dryer. Through the lone window I watch the mauve shadows of the winter afternoon move over the snow that still covers the yard, and I try to appreciate the beauty and stillness. We moved to this quiet street in this quiet town to get away from the city, but especially from an apartment thick with memories of a dead mother, and, yes, a dead wife. It was my husband's decision, and knowing that it loosened the constriction that fear had wrapped him in, I consented. Having never had a child of my own, I could only imagine the heartache he felt, thinking that he was failing his only one.

In the kitchen I hear that the repetitive notes of the technical exercises have been replaced by the Haydn scherzo, one of the pieces assigned for the week. The child plays it hesitantly, although she has practiced it daily. I tell myself it's the combination of pianissimo and speed in the middle section that causes her trouble, but I know it isn't that, but those tense hands that refuse to relax even for this woman whom she wants to please.

The teacher came to us highly recommended by the school. She gives the lessons here, because her apartment isn't suitable she says, offering tales of a wily mouse and failed heat. She shows up, invariably late, in a sedan that appears neither safe nor dependable. Her health is a cause of concern, not that she seems contagious; she alludes to bouts of migraine, asthma, gastritis. She speaks of her husband and of how his shifting moods, bursts of anger, and inability to communicate are stretching the fabric of their marriage. She speaks softly, with a troubling absence of affect, usually in reply to my greeting, the casual, "How are you?" I try to remember not to use these words. I don't want to peer into her private life, an unwitting Peeping Tom. I sympathize but try to steer the conversation down more positive avenues, as her appetite for self-pity seems bottomless.

The second hand on the clock above the sink advances with audible ticks that bridge the hesitant notes coming from the living room. Otherwise, there is silence—a quiet room in a quiet house on a quiet street in a quiet town. How I miss the city. But this is a secret that I hug to myself, knowing that it would only add to my husband's shoulder-load of cares and contribute nothing to the well-being of our family. The piano teacher has spoken of her husband's refusal to open up to her, but I mistrust this rush to self-revelation, this need to confess one's every misstep that fills our magazines and airways.

The Lab lifts his heavy blond head, his eyes still dreamy with sleep, and grumbles deep in his chest. Reaching for the tea kettle, I pause. I'm expecting no one. Perhaps it's a delivery. But, no, the dog lowers his head, asleep before it reaches his paws. I have no visitors, only the piano teacher. Gone are my city friends and my busy schedule. I pour the hot water over a tea bag and, leaving it to cool, go to the front door to check. Night is edging in; I switch on the outside lights before returning to the kitchen. In the living room the lamp beside the piano shines on the teacher and her pupil.

The cup of tea has cooled enough to allow for tentative sips. Perhaps I will bake gingerbread, my stepdaughter's favorite, for tonight's dessert. Finding what pleases her is a challenge, for she seems to need so little and asks for almost nothing.

The piano falls silent, signaling that the lesson is drawing to a close, that the following week's assignments are being explained, and I pause in lifting the canister of flour from the shelf, and wait. It comes. The house, with its wide empty spaces, is filled with sound, an explosion of lightning runs, each note full and mellow and articulated despite the speed achieved by the piano teacher's flying fingers. For the length of the piece, I imagine her ills, her husband's tantrums, even her disappointments, are swallowed up by the breath-stopping beauty of her music.

I have questioned her about playing professionally. Her explanations are rambling tales of a cold and demanding mother who taught her to play only hymns, and of dreams stifled by the pressure of financial need. The piece ends, and the house is quiet again. With the flour canister pressed to my chest, I walk out to the foyer in time to see the teacher and her pupil saying their good-byes. Stirred by the lesson, their faces shine as though lit from within. I hold the door for the piano teacher. As she leaves, she assures the child that she'll return the following week.

The End

SOMEDAY YOU'LL UNDERSTAND

M Y NAME is Melanie Jane Flowers, and I'm eight years old, and I'm writing this story so if they find me dead you can tell the police who did it. My mother. "Melanie, I'm going to kill you!" Those are the exact words she said to me in our kitchen where we live at 38 Stelfox Street, Aspinhill, New Jersey, at 9:30 p.m. on February 15, 2005.

What I think is, she's getting really violent in her middle age. First she threw Daddy out of our house, and then she threw Aunt Sue out, who is her very own sister and who used to live with us. Now she is threatening my life.

Cindy, my teacher, said we can write about whatever we choose in creative writing as long as she says it's okay. That doesn't sound like whatever we choose, but she said my subject was okay, so I'm not going to argue. Something I do too much of, according to my mother, but my dad says cool it a little and I'll make a great lawyer. Too bad. I already decided to be a vet. Dogs love me.

You are probably wondering why my mother is going to kill me. One reason is she doesn't think before she talks is what Daddy says. Not like I do. I would never tell someone, especially a poor little child, that I was going to kill them. Although I might think it, but if you say it out loud, your words may come back to haunt you. My Aunt Sue taught me that. I miss her, because she used to bake us special cakes and watch TV with me. Not like my mother, who's always at work or spending all her time on Uncle Bob. Who, in case you're wondering, is not my real uncle, a good thing, but since the divorce he's here a lot of the time, a bad thing.

The next reason my mother wants to kill me is she got called into school by Cindy and the principal, and she had to miss work, and she says it gives her a bad reputation in her office if she has to keep running to my school all the time. Which she doesn't, this was only the second time. Maybe the third. Anyhow, she had to come in because I locked myself in the paste closet and wouldn't come out. But I did it so I wouldn't lose control and smash Frankie Cloakey in his hideous freckled face, after he said my mother was a bad woman (I can't write the word he called her or Cindy will say it's not appropriate for a story and x it out). Anyhow, it's none of Frankie's business how many times Uncle Bob's red truck parks in front of our house, and now I wish I'd belted him.

So you can maybe understand my mom wasn't thinking I was the daughter she'd always dreamed of when reason number three happened. It was that I told Daddy that Uncle Bob walks around with no pants on. Very gross. That's all I can say about the gross part, because Cindy xed out what I wrote first. But she said I <u>could</u> say I'm really, really happy I'm a girl, not a boy.

Actually, my mother always says to be honest, especially with yourself, and I want this story to be true I'm a little bit sorry I told my dad about Uncle Bob and his bareness. First of all, he only did it once, and he only did it by accident, because he didn't know I was there. And second of all it made him even sadder than before—my dad, not Uncle Bob. Something I didn't know at first when he completely lost it. He called his lawyer, and he called Mommy, and he yelled and yelled. If you knew him, you'd know he doesn't usually yell—like a certain person in our family does.

After she promised to kill me, and she wasn't in her extremely pissed off mood, Mommy told me, "Some day, Melanie, you'll understand." But I am doubtful.

I was hoping Daddy would let me stay with him and Aunt Sue in the apartment they got when Mommy threw them out. It's not very big. It's only got one bedroom, but I could sleep on the couch. At least I wouldn't be being killed. But he said no. He says my chances of living to a ripe old age are very good. Like I said, I'm doubtful. That's why I wrote this story.

And now I'm going to write a moral, because my favorite stories have them at the end.

Moral: Don't ever try to get even with your mother, especially after you locked yourself in a paste closet.

THE END

BE CAREFUL WHAT YOU WISH FOR

THE BASKET of clothes seemed bottomless. As Audrey removed another pair of overalls, immersing them in the tub of soapy water, she prayed for the hundredth time that morning that the repairman would arrive as promised before noon. Scrubbing the knees of the pants, she glanced beside her at the growing pile on top the useless washing machine and tried to decide if she had enough clothes for the children, who were romping around, perfectly happy in their underpants and nothing else. A strand of wayward hair insisted on falling over her eyes, causing her to stop swishing the pants in order to brush the hair back. From overhead came a jarring yell and the sound of a herd of wild horses—or four little boys—racing through the dining room above her. The social worker from Children's Aid was due at one that afternoon.

It had started out innocently enough. She would borrow the child for just a few hours, the length of Godiva's visit, no longer. It would be doing the mother a favor, wouldn't it? As well as giving the little thing the attention she sadly seemed to be lacking. For her own part, Audrey would have, if only for a few hours, the beautiful girl-child she'd always wanted, the baby Rosie she'd bragged about in her Christmas letter to Godiva. How was she to know that her former roommate's unexpected visit would set off such a life-changing series of events? She wasn't, of course, and right there was the proof of her good intentions.

They'd been roommates their freshman year at Montclair State, she and Godiva and Ruthie O'Dwyer. Only Ruthie went on to graduate. Godiva left after that first year and immediately headed for Los Angeles, where she lived to this day. She'd appeared in several B films, been an extra in one of Clint Eastwood's <u>Dirty Harry</u> films, and married three times that Audrey knew of, thanks to marriage and divorce announcements Godiva and her intended, or ex, sent out. The latter had stunned her. So . . . civilized, she supposed.

Audrey herself had lasted through her sophomore year before leaving to marry Caz, a decision she'd never regretted. Big, burly Caz remained as sweet and understanding as he'd been on the day they exchanged their vows. The only sour note in their years together was their childlessness, which weighed more heavily on Audrey as she approached menopause and the finality of it all.

The three former friends exchanged occasional Christmas and birthday cards—birth announcements from Ruthie—and that was about it. In her Christmas notes the previous year, stumped for something to say, she'd told Godiva and Ruthie about her little girl—who, sadly, didn't exist—never thinking she'd see either of the roommates again in this life. And here was Godiva, proposing a visit.

> <u>Coming east for my niece's weding. Out to Aspenhill next Sat. early aft. Can't wait to see you—also Rosie!</u> Godiva had e-mailed.

What had ever possessed her to make up such a story? Audrey asked herself as she went about tidying the house, not that it required much in the way of tidying. It took little effort to keep a house without children immaculate.

The child, Sammy—she guessed for Samantha—lived in a ramshackle dwelling behind the vet's office where Audrey worked. She'd shown up in the waiting room asking to see the puppies, thumb in mouth and beautiful despite a smeary face and grimy, threadbare overalls. Audrey couldn't resist. She'd taken the chubby hand the child held out with endearing eagerness and led her to the rear of the building where there were always boarder dogs in residence. The little thing had hunkered down near the cages and whispered what sounded like gibberish to Audrey but must have been meaningful to the dogs, who responded with soft moans and fluttering tails. The next day she was back, and the next and the next.

At first Audrey had stayed with her, but as the days went on she took to leaving her while she went about her duties. Apparently Sammy was never missed, which was mildly alarming to Audrey, who always made sure she got home. She would watch the child take an unhurried, crooked path through the high grass that separated the animal clinic from the yard surrounding the shabby house she disappeared into. Part way home, she always stopped and turned to wave to Audrey, who hated to send her from the sparkling cleanliness of the clinic to the house with the grimy windows, torn shades, and broken screen door, the house that sat amid a sea of junk and rusting cars.

She planned carefully for Godiva's visit, reviewing each step until the Saturday in question played smoothly in her mind. Caz had been dropping hints about the opening of hunting season, which was to be, as luck would have it, on that very Saturday. Assuring him that she and Godiva would spend the afternoon catching up on one another's lives freed him from the guilt he usually saddled himself with when he went hunting. He'd be out of the house by five a.m. and gone until darkness set in around six p.m. By then, Godiva would be long gone, and Audrey would have Sammy back home.

She worked until noon on Saturday. Sammy came late in the morning to see the puppies. Audrey planned to leave with her through the back door. The promise of seeing another puppy, Audrey and Caz's dog Gunner, would be enough, she was sure, to get the little girl into her car. She had debated buying a car seat for the five-mile trip home but decided against it. Instead she'd found a booster seat at K-Mart that should keep Sammy safe.

When she pulled into the driveway and saw Caz's Subaru, she should have known right then that the day wasn't going to proceed as she'd imagined; should have turned around and taken Sammy home. But, no, she eased to a stop and turned with a big smile to the little girl.

"Here we are, Pumpkin, and look—here comes the puppy." She pointed to the yellow Lab loping toward the car.

Released from the back seat, Sammy embraced Gunner, jabbering a stream of gibberish, while Audrey faced Caz, who came limping out the side door wearing his canvas hunting jacket and a puzzled frown.

"Meet Sammy, Caz," she said, adding hastily, "I'm watching her for a few hours . . . for her folks. What happened to you? You're limping."

A smile as wide as his face had replaced the frown, as Caz limped past her and bent over Sammy and Gunner. "Hello, little fellow. You like dogs, do you? I can see Gunner sure likes you."

Audrey began to breathe again. Of course, it would be okay. She'd forgotten how much Caz loved children. He was leading Sammy by the hand toward the house before she thought to say, "She's a girl." But Caz, deep in a conversation about dogs, didn't hear her.

"I think he needs a good cleaning up," Caz said as they all entered the kitchen. He frowned at Audrey, blame implicit in his tone of voice. "What'd you let him get into?"

"Yes, I know—she needs a bath and a fresh diaper." She held up the box of Huggies she'd bought earlier in the week and stored in her car. "But what happened to your leg?"

He waved an impatient hand. "The old knee gave out again, so I quit for the day. Want me to dunk him in the tub?" He pointed at Sammy, who was chasing after a disappearing Gunner.

"Oh, would you? That'd be a big help—Godiva's due any minute. Here are clean clothes," she said, handing him a shopping bag. "And, Caz—he's a she. Samantha."

"Huh! You'd never know it under all that dirt." He followed the dog and child parade out of the kitchen, and she heard him clumping up the steps, one at a time, talking about bubble baths.

Audrey pushed down the frantic feeling welling up in her at the thought of Caz hearing Godiva call Sammy "Rosie," the fictitious name she'd given the fictitious child in her Christmas card. She had to carry on and was putting the finishing touches on a tray of teacups and plates of cakes and cookies when she heard a car in the driveway. She made it to the front stoop in time to see Godiva emerge from the back seat of a Lincoln Town Car. First came a substantial leg, gleaming in a sheer stocking, the foot shod in a four-inch heeled sandal, all thin, iridescent straps. Next came a hip, quickly followed by one bare arm and the torso, clad in a swirl of turquoise silk. Finally, Godiva's canary-yellow head dipped under the rim of the car door. With the aid of her other arm, she dragged out the matching leg and hip, then settled all the various body parts into their accustomed places with an energetic shimmy, impressive in its execution. Waving to Audrey, "I'm here!" she cried in a voice that flowed out over the neighborhood, before reaching into the car to produce a fur stole, which she wrapped around her shoulders. "Can you believe it?" Her head flew back with the force of her laughter that seemed to well up from the pit of her stomach.

Audrey forgot her anxiety for a moment and joined in. All these years, she thought, and I'd forgotten the infectiousness of that laugh. She watched Godiva navigate the walk and steps, marveling that the two wispy sandals supported her weight, and happily endured the bear hug that went on and on.

". . . so good to see you," she managed on the little breath left her, as she led the way to the living room.

They were deep into reminiscing when Caz appeared carrying a Sammy Audrey barely recognized. The little girl's face, scrubbed clean and freed from straggling hair, was cherubic, framed by damp, freshly shampooed white curls. The only discordant note was the overalls, the same ones she'd been wearing before Caz bathed her, not the newly purchased pink corduroy pair from the shopping bag.

"Here she is!" Godiva cried. "Oh, such a gorgeous baby! Come see your Aunt Godiva! That's a sweetie," she cooed, bending over and extending her arms to an agreeable Sammy, who, set on her feet by Caz, ran straight into them.

Audrey crossed the room to Caz. "Why did you put those old overalls on her?" she hissed.

"Her's a him," he growled. "Damned if I'm going to put him in pink." He walked over to Godiva. "Hello, Godiva, I'm Caz. Heard a lot about you over the years. But I guess you two have lots of catching up to do, so f'you'll excuse me, I'll go upstairs. Got a bum leg that needs resting."

A laughing Godiva momentarily interrupted swinging Sammy in circles to acknowledge his greeting. Audrey found herself unable to move. A "him"? Sammy really was Sammy, not Samantha? She watched Godiva collapse on the sofa with him on her lap.

"Oh, Auddie, your baby's adorable!" She hugged Sammy to her heaving breast. "Yes, you are. Adorable. What fun this is! Oh, I'm so glad I came."

The parking area behind the animal clinic was empty when Audrey pulled in at a little past four. She barely had the strength to cut the wheel. Her arms like the rest of her felt limp and ineffectual. She was about to turn to Sammy with reassurances that he could see Gunner again real soon—he'd put up such a fuss when it'd been time to leave the dog—when she realized that something was wrong. Several police cars, topbars rotating red, white, and blue beams, were parked at the house behind the clinic.

"Oh, God, no!" she cried aloud. Sammy had been missed. Of course he had. Had she been mad thinking he could be gone since morning with no one noticing? Panic drained whatever strength she had left, following an afternoon fraught with the fear of Caz reappearing and her scheme revealed for the lie it was. Finally, she'd been unable to contain the waves of anxiety that had her hands shaking and her knees turning to liquid, and she'd confessed everything to a startled Godiva. Bless her, Godiva'd risen to the occasion, administering another rib-crushing bear hug along with reassurances of her complete understanding, being childless herself, and sympathy that Sammy was only on loan.

But now it was no longer being viewed as an innocent borrowing on Audrey's part. Now she was being sought for kidnapping. Her picture on tomorrow's front page with the headline, "Local Woman Steals Child," was only one of the images that began flashing through her mind.

"Bubby! Bubby! Hi, Bubby!" Sammy cried, kicking excited heels against the seat and knocking a tattoo on the car window.

Audrey looked out the side window to see a boy—no, several boys—crawling out of the tall grass and heading to the car.

"Sammy!" they cried, "Hey! Sammy!" And then they were all scrambling into the back seat. Three very dirty little boys of varying ages.

"Hello," Audrey ventured. "And who have we here?" They grew still, scrambling back on the seat and on one another, gazing at her with surprise written on their gritty faces. The largest of the crew, who looked to be seven or eight, put an arm around Sammy and murmured, "I'm Timmy."

Audrey nodded. "I see," for she did. Timmy's resemblance to Sammy was impossible to miss. "Are you Sammy's brother?"

"Uh-huh." Pointing to the others, he added, "Me and them—we're brothers."

Timmy's hair was no longer white, probably sandy brown, she guessed, if it were clean. And his curls were relaxed and not as thick as Sammy's. But the four occupants of the back seat were definitely family.

"I see policemen at your house," she said.

Timmy looked wary. "Uh-huh."

"I guess they want Sammy."

"Sammy?" Timmy forgot his shyness and looked at her as though she weren't especially bright. "No, they got Daddy. They said he got a warren, and he's gotta go to jail." He paused before admitting, "I listened through the back window."

A warren? "A warrant?"

"Yeah," a smaller brother chimed in. "And Timmy made us run, so's they wouldn't get us, 'cause—"

Timmy shushed the brother who'd spoken, and, as family patriarch, continued, "'cause they're gonna take my mom, too, 'cause she got drugs."

"Your mother? Has drugs?"

Timmy nodded vigorously. "Yeah, she's a druggie, Daddy says. He says that's why he gotta steal the cars 'n all."

At the sound of engines being revved, Audrey turned and saw that the police cars were driving away. She looked across the expanse of grass and mud at the house, unlit and forlorn in the growing dusk.

"Who's there, Timmy? Who's going to take care of you?"

"Ain't nobody." He chewed on his lower lip. "Maybe we can go with you and Sammy?" he asked.

"Nobody? Surely the police—someone—will make arrangements? They won't leave you alone . . . I'm sure they won't."

The children sat very still. The other two looked to be kindergarten age and must have been twins. They watched Timmy, who in turn stared at Audrey.

"We hid," he said, breaking the silence. "'cause we don't wanna have to go with the cops like last time, 'cause they take us to different places. 'cause they called us 'wards-a-tate,' and my mom says, 'Fuck that.' So maybe we can go with you and Sammy." He gazed at her, mouth slightly open, lower lip trembling. "Please?"

THE END

FAITH AND HOPE

A T 9:10 a.m. on a Wednesday in late March, Alice Croneberg walked into the United Mercantile Bank on West Main Street, withdrawal slip folded neatly in her wallet. Across the marble foyer the bullet-proof glass of the teller windows shone in the day's weak light, allowing her to see who was working that morning. She decided to go to the young teller with the helmet of unnaturally red hair, thinking she would be the least likely to be interested in Alice's business. The other two were old timers who might make some comment on the amount of the withdrawal.

Her heels made a loud clip clop as she approached the window, making her presence noticeable—she'd hoped to slip in and out, business quickly and quietly transacted. Was everyone watching her? She gave herself a figurative shake and placed her handbag on the ledge. Paranoia needed to be stopped before it took over, she reminded herself. Digging into the bag for her wallet, she smiled pleasantly at the teller and, with a light push she slid a slip of paper with the checking account number on it into the dip in the ledge that the bank had cleverly engineered to make the glass shield appear but a design feature, not the necessary safety measure it was. The young woman studied it, then raised bored eyes before turning to the computer. Her long cherry red tipped fingers moved rapidly on the keyboard. Her face was expressionless as she jotted a figure on the paper and returned it to Alice. Irritated that Howard must have paid the mortgage early but relieved that he hadn't taken out for the quarterly tax bill or car insurance, Alice wrote a check for $6,400, leaving a balance of $27.92.

At 9:30 she was standing on the sidewalk in front of the bank, letting the rising wind out of the west cool her face. By 9:45 she was on the turnpike, headed south to Atlantic City. Lowering the driver's side window several inches and filling her lungs in the gush of cold air, she felt as though more than her chest was expanding, six months worth of stifling existence was lifting off her shoulders and flowing into the New Jersey atmosphere.

Once past the congestion of the city and the industrial northern flank of the pike, she could actually feel the pull of the tables, the car cutting through air like a ship through water, and wished all her cares and misgivings could be left in its wake. Chief among them, her job, although if it lasted another six weeks, she'd be surprised. Not that she minded, because she hated it, hated the humorless, mindless people and the dull, dehumanizing routine. But Howard—how would she explain getting the ax twice in one year to him? Howard, who'd worked for the same firm he'd joined right out of college, would not be amused.

Around her, the deepening gray of the trees and grass was nearly one with the sky, and she felt the tug of the wheel as the car argued with a strong gust of wind. Soon fat drops of rain began to bounce off the windshield.

"Great—glad you can make it on such short notice . . . no, nothing special. Alice and I thought getting the old crowd together might take our minds off this God-awful weather we've been having."

When he finished on the phone, Howard Croneberg poured himself a cup of coffee and sank into his recliner, determined to enjoy the day away from the office. Later he'd consult the list on the refrigerator door for the name of the Chinese restaurant that he and Alice liked. He'd order the dinners early, so they'd deliver, but he'd have to go to the bakery for the dessert. He'd considered ordering a sheet cake but decided against it, because what could he have had written on it? <u>Congratulations on Your Six Month Anniversary</u>? Hardly, yet he knew how difficult those months had been for her—going to meetings, showing up at the office every day, finding new ways to use her spare time. Hope and faith, he'd told her, they'll get us through the hard times.

It was close to three when she backed away from the table. She fumbled for a handkerchief to blot her face, the room suddenly unbearably hot, and felt her hands shaking. Lord, it had been going so well—the smoky warmth of the Scotch in her mouth and the unbelievable rush she'd felt each time she pulled in more chips—and then this. And she hadn't called Howard. It was too noisy, too goddamn noisy, that was the problem—she could barely think. She thrust her hands into her jacket pockets. The important thing, the thing she had to concentrate on, was that she hadn't lost it all. She hadn't lost it all, and she had time—as long as she was home by seven. So what she needed to do was to call Howard . . . and let him know her day was going just fine.

Howard smiled what he hoped was a "relaxed host" sort of smile at Ben Faraday, who was at the counter, helping out by filling drink orders. Spooning globs of moo shu pork onto a plate, he prayed his stomach wouldn't betray him. Christ! Chinese food wasn't the thing to handle when your insides were acting like they were on a ship in high seas. Where was she? Too late to call her office it would just go to message. Maybe he should be checking the local hospitals, but he knew that wasn't right. Fucking hell!

The doorbell chimed—probably the Kahns able to make it after all. Ben signaled he'd answer it. Howard threw the serving spoon into the sink, wiped his hands on a towel already sticky with various sauces and pieces of rice, and slid the plastic lid off a container of sesame noodles.

"I know, I know, I'm late—oh, my lord! This kitchen's a disaster." Alice dropped her raincoat on a chair, kissed him on the mouth before he could say a word, and began to organize the counter. In a matter of minutes she'd supplied him with clean spoons, stacked the unused plates, set the filled ones on the table, found a fresh garbage bag, and dumped the empty cartons.

He began, "Where the hell—"

"Later, I'll tell you later. Right now let's get our guests fed." She grinned at him, her eyes a little wild, her voice husky with excitement.

Howard thought the night would never end, but, of course, it finally did, and their friends made their way to their cars after lingering good nights.

He closed the door and leaned against itThe stairs to the second floor lay ahead of him; the living room with the dining area beyond it was to his right. This was the fifth home he and Alice had occupied in eleven years, each one less grand than the one it succeeded. Still, the clean-up after a party remained daunting, no matter the size of the rooms. And waiting for attention were smudged glasses, coffee cups atilt in their saucers, crumpled napkins, and in the kitchen, a sink and counter piled with food-caked plates and cutlery and too many serving dishes of leftover Chinese food needing refrigeration or the garbage can.

He left the support of the door and made his way to the kitchen, gathering up as many glasses as he could on the way, ignoring the slumbering form of his wife in one of the large club chairs.

It was long past midnight when he finished by putting the garbage in the can at the bottom of the back steps. After fastening the handles, he dragged it out front for the morning collection, the screech of the rusty wheels disturbing the early morning silence. The air was crisp, washed clean by the earlier storm, and he paused at the curb for a moment. Overhead, a quarter moon was hurrying across the sky, obscured here and there by dark bursts of cloud. Gazing at the hunched shapes of darkened houses, he thought of the neighbors, most of whom he knew only by sight, not name, having only lived on Stelfox for a few months. A remnant of the storm's wind stirred, chilling the air, and he retraced his steps.

The kitchen stood at attention, almost as neat as the day they'd moved in. Upstairs he was going to pack only the bare essentials. He knew the chances were good Alice would sleep in the chair until morning. "Look at this, sweetheart," she'd said, thrusting a handbag stuffed with bills at him. Well, so much for faith . . . and hope, too.

He moved through the downstairs, dimming lights, the sound of her breathing loud in the still rooms. Pain was blossoming like a rogue weed in his chest, but he shrugged it off. If he took the last of the money in the mutual fund account, he could cover the tax bill. Maybe he'd pay the car insurance in installments.

THE END

I'M SENDING YOU AN ANGEL

TRAFFIC STUTTERS along Cedar Street, horns emitting sharp barks of protest. Morning rush hour is at its peak, the distant wail of sirens only adding to drivers' anxiety. Dora hesitates at the corner of Seventeenth and looks east, to where Cedar has become a pinpoint of flashing lights. She doesn't know anyone from that side of town to worry about, but the hospital is down there. Trouble, she thinks. It's everywhere. But not, she hopes where all them sick people be.

Stepping off the curb, she picks her way between bumpers, trying to keep her loose cardigan from flapping in the wind. The light is green for the cross street, still the intersection is filled with cars, the drivers tight-faced and frustrated by the bottleneck. You has to be careful, she knows, look right at them to make sure they sees you. Once on the other side, she continues along Seventeenth to Grand to the bus stop, planting each foot in its thick black oxford with due deliberation, shifting heavy hips to balance the weight of the cumbersome tote bag she carries.

At the end of the block, she's relieved to see that both the small shelter and the bench are empty. "Praise be, thank you, Jesus," she murmurs, lowering herself onto the green plastic seat. Working a tissue out of a side pocket of her dress, she dabs a face the color of seasoned walnut and glowing with perspiration despite the cool Autumn wind. The dress, fashioned from a lustrous purple fabric, has ridden up over her considerable knees, revealing a second dress, this one of black jersey. Its high neckline has escaped the restraint of the synthetic purple to form a fringe of wilted ruffles under her chin. Heaving the bag onto her lap, she digs through it and extracts a Bible from a tangle of underwear.

Her fingers skim through the pages. "Isaiah," she murmurs, "Isaiah one, verse four." She begins in a hoarse whisper, "'O sinful nation, people loaded with iniquity, race of evildoers, wanton destructive children who have deserted the Lord . . .'"

Joann Godwin eases her Volvo wagon to the curb in front of James Madison Elementary School, having waited until the fire truck leaving the driveway has crossed in front of her and nosed into the downhill traffic creeping toward the center of town.

"See? See, Mum, there is a fire!" Justin kicks the back of her seat in his excitement. "No school! No school!" he chants. The girls join him in thin, shrill soprano voices. "No school! No school!"

"Calm down, all of you!" Joann cries. "There is school. The fire truck's gone—see? No smoke. Out you go, and don't forget your packs." She watches them grumble their way onto the sidewalk and fall in with a wave of equally disappointed children who are scuffing at the leaves that litter the walk and poking at one another as they drag themselves toward the main entrance. Ordinarily, she'd have continued on to the high school, where she teaches freshman lit. But, it's Wednesday, Dora's day to clean, and she's taken the day off. Since the summer months, when she was home while Dora cleaned, she's known it would come down to this.

"You getting on or just sitting there?"

Dora looks up. The 84 has pulled to the curb, and the driver's face, ripe with irritation, is leaning toward the open door.

"Yessir, thank you, sir. I'm coming, yes, yes,I am." Clutching the Bible in one hand, tote bag in the other, she pulls herself up the high steps into the bus. Huffing to catch her breath, her bosom rising and falling at an alarming rate, she pushes a bill into the fare box and, at a lurch of the bus, falls into the closest seat, where she sits, Bible open on her lap, until the bus approaches Stelfox.

"Thank you, sir, God bless you," she says to the driver, oblivious to his frown, as she waits for the doors to swing open.

She's been making the walk along Stelfox to the Godwins' house for close on ten years. Every other Wednesday, not that all her days are taken. She pushes the thought of lost jobs aside. The Lord has ways of testing His believers, she knows that. And she isn't going to question any of those ways, no, sir. He has his reasons. And didn't He send her to Missus

Godwin? Bless her, there's a lady who understands, a real Christian lady, Missus Godwin is.

Joann is standing at the front window and watching Dora approach. She's never seen the woman hurry, moving as though to music, taking in the sights around her as she advances. And no matter the season or temperature, her head is clad in a close-fitting crocheted hat that covers almost all of her hair, leaving only a fringe of shiny gray curls. Joann sighs. She knows so much about her cleaning woman—and so little. She knows that Dora is trustworthy, but she has no idea if the woman can separate reality from fantasy. She certainly knows about her living arrangements, and the thought of these stirs another sigh.

"In here," she calls out, swinging the front door open. "Come in this way. It's getting chilly—I think it's the wind."

Dora bobs her head in agreement. "Yes, ma'am, yes, ma'am. Winter be here before we know it, and that's the truth."

In the laundry room, she clunks the heavy tote bag onto the floor and collects the necessary cleaning supplies, arranging them in a plastic pail. Pail in hand, she hefts the vacuum and mounts the stairs to the second floor: "Yes, Lord, oh, yes, Lord, I'm comin', Lord, I'm comin'."

Joann winces. She decides to wash clothes, knowing that from the laundry room, she won't have to listen to Dora's one-way conversation with God. She assumes it's one-way, but what does she know? Perhaps . . . she gives her head a shake. The whole thing is beyond her.

To get to the washing machine, she has to step around Dora's tote bag. The size of a small suitcase, Joann notices that its sides have expanded since the summer. Giving in to what she prefers to think of as curiosity, not nosiness, she spreads the opening with hesitant fingers. Dismay seizes her. Embedded in a pile of underclothing and heavy stockings is a cluster of disparate articles—she can see a banana, a packet of envelopes held by a grimy rubber band, and a small, empty picture frame, and, wedged into side pockets, a black leather change purse, a Bible, and a tube of Colgate toothpaste.

Over the summer Joann listened to tales Dora recounted of the harassment she was enduring from her landlady and the woman's teenage children in their effort to get her to leave the room she rents in their home in Port Smith. Joann has never seen the house in the poor, heavily populated part of town, but from the description, it's ill-kept and badly in need of repair. She listened with equal parts indignation and disbelief to how Dora's food had been contaminated, how clothing was stolen from her bureau and closet, how music was blasted at all hours of the night. Dora claimed that her fear of a fire kept her awake most nights. But Joann has to wonder—would the landlady burn down her own house to rid herself of a tenant?

From overhead comes the roar of the vacuum and the occasional thump as it wings the side of a door or a corner of furniture. Joann's used to the sounds. She knows that what Dora lacks in the finer points of house cleaning, she makes up for with a commendable enthusiasm for her work.

By noon, having transformed the baskets of dirty laundry into neat stacks of folded clothes and linens, she interrupts Dora, who's attacking the dust in the family room. "I'm going to warm up last night's beef stew for my lunch. There's plenty, and it will just go to waste—won't you help me eat it?" It has to be on those terms. Food that will otherwise be thrown out is acceptable, while a sandwich prepared expressly for Dora will be refused. The issue is charity, and Joann understands that, but it makes offering anything to this woman, who so clearly needs help, a challenge . . . and, she thinks, really not my responsibility.

Dora looks at her from across the room, eyes like overly bright blackberries, narrowed in suspicion. "You sure the kids won't eat it?" she asks.

"No, I promised them pizza for dinner. I'll fix us both a plate, all right?"

"Yes, ma'am, that be fine, then."

"They related to the police chief, you know," Dora announces as she butters a sourdough roll that Joann has heated.

"Your landlady?"

Dora nods, vigorously chewing a chunk of roll. Swallowing, she continues, "She says I'm breakin' a san'tation law, havin' me a refrigerator. Says she gonna report it to the health department."

Joann looks at her, despair ruining the lunch she's trying to eat. "Oh, Dora, I'm sure . . ." Her voice trails off. For the truth is, she's no longer sure of anything where Dora's concerned.

"Gonna be okay. The good Lord <u>provides</u> for his angels, and I got my dreams, yes, ma'am, I got my dreams. He tells me, 'Dora, you're one of my own, one of my bless ones, you're an angel.'" She fixes Joann with shining eyes. "Yes, ma'am, I'm an angel." Bending over her plate, she wipes up the last of the gravy with a swipe of her roll.

"Well . . ."

"I put myself in Jesus' hands. Oh, yes, He takes care of his angels, yes, He takes care of us. I know that, I know my Lord gonna take care of me."

Dora's voice has achieved a rhythm that requires no reply, other than 'Amen, Sister,' a response not encouraged by Joann's fellow Presbyterians. The solutions she's been able to come up with in an effort to fix the problem—contacting Port Smith's Department of Social Services, poring over classified ads in search of a room for rent that Dora might feasibly be able to afford, persuading friends and colleagues to have her clean for them—have ended as exercises in failure, leaving her frustrated, and both angry and sad.

Dora is rocking in her chair, her round face—which Joann believes had been molded along lines of sweetness and humor—is creased into a mask of suffering and emitting the fire of a zealot, as she continues, "Got us a job to do, us angels. Those folks gonna be sorry, they're gonna be sorry they run me out. Oh, yes, Lord, they be <u>weeping</u>! Jesus say in Matthew 13, ' . . . the angels, they'll separate wicked from good and throw them into the <u>blazing furnace</u>!'"

These last two words have been delivered so fervently that Joann feels any residual hope she may have been nursing turn to ash, as though it's gone into the furnace along with the landlady and her brood.

After lunch she retreats to the second floor with the basket of clean laundry. As she stacks towels and sheets in the linen closet, she reminds herself that her first duty is to her children. Their safety has to come first, and how safe is a woman who believes, who <u>fervently</u> believes, she's an angel? By two o'clock she's ready. She finds Dora stowing the vacuum attachments on the shelf next to the dryer.

"Dora . . . we need to talk." Somehow she gets the words out. Keeping her eyes on the fluttering ruffle of black jersey at Dora's chin, she speaks rapidly, breathlessly, speaks of doing the housework herself, of appreciating all that Dora has done, of how very, very sorry she is. And somehow she steels herself to ignore the resignation in the cleaning woman's voice. Oh, God, she thinks—anger, even a curse from Isaiah, anything but resignation. She stuffs three one-hundred dollar bills into the hand that isn't grasping the tote bag, opens the back door, and waits for the Lord's angel to go on her way.

The End

MAKE BELIEVE

===

Eddie had died like a firecracker going off, quickly, noisily, and attracting lots of attention. He would have liked that, Jenna thought. Of course, he had no way of knowing that the package delivered to his lab that autumn afternoon would explode, tearing the lab—and him-—into a million pieces.

She and Eddie had been married forty years, right out of college. It had taken eighteen months for her to come to terms with his death. Not that she had expected him to walk into the house and resume their life together, no, but the number of times she'd found herself silently reviewing the events of a day in anticipation of relating them to him had greatly diminished. And it was only recently that she had been able to open his closet door and think about disposing of his clothes without a sob escaping her.

Eddie had died in October, and Jenna had continued to work until the following summer. Then, at sixty-one, she'd decided it was time to retire, feeling, as she was, the weight of caring for a large house on her own. Besides, she'd had, in addition to Eddie's pension and their savings, a great deal of insurance money. Money wasn't the problem. The problem, Jenna was forced to admit, was her fantasy life. Even thinking the words made her wince.

Asked to describe herself, she would have placed 'sensible' at the forefront of adjectives. 'Down-to-earth,' 'sane,' 'two feet planted firmly on the ground,' these were descriptive of her. She was, after all, an editor of non-fiction.

Eddie, successful in medical research, had been the shooting star, and she had been content to stand in his shadow and keep the show going. She had raised the children, walked the dogs, balanced the checkbook, filled the Christmas stockings, sat up with the feverish child. There had been no time for fantasies.

Was that it? she wondered. That time was suddenly something she could fashion to <u>her</u> liking, not to the needs of others. Or could it be her own hated, fast-approaching sixty-fifth birthday—death looming? Whatever it was, she was still sane enough to recognize that a fantasy world posed a problem. And her sanity was a concern. For a sixty-three year-old woman to spend her waking hours living a dream life with a thirty-something man—wasn't that crossing the border of neurosis? In her fantasy, she was thirty-nine, a desirable age with none of the callowness of youth and all the maturity of years, yet none of their baggage. A few wrinkles perhaps, but only the kind that lent character and interest to a face.

When Eddie died, it seemed everyone had been eager to advise her about what to do with the rest of her life.

"A cruise, dear. You need to get away from all the familiar sights and sounds."

"Come and stay with us, Mother. The extra bedroom is yours, and you know how you love the city."

"Get a cat, Jenna, as soon as possible. A cat is so therapeutic. At the very least, a dog."

"Don't change a thing, Jen. Stay here on Stelfox Street."

She had changed very little, but found that almost everything in her life had changed a great deal. On really bad days, when she was unable to fix herself a meal, let alone work on an assignment, she'd gone next door to sit in the kitchen of a neighbor who had lost her husband in a plane crash. Liz had let her sit as long as she needed, known that she didn't require sympathy or bright chatter or wise advice, only another person's presence close by for the time it took to work through a particular grief.

She had been ready to recycle the flyer listing fall courses at the community college when one of the offerings caught her eye: <u>Drawing on the Right Side of the Brain/Tues. Thurs.10am/Richard Cayman,MFA</u>. How strange. Eddie had often chided her about being too left-brained. "You need to write some fiction, take an art course, stir up the right side of your brain," he had said more than once. A plan of action for Tuesdays and Thursdays was certainly something she could use. She registered for the course.

"Good morning." He stood before them in a shaft of September sunlight knifing in through tall windows. With raven hair swept back from a wide brow and dark eyes that drilled into each student in turn, he commanded attention.

"You are beautiful, unique human beings, each of you an individual worth knowing and loving," he announced in a voice tailor-made for hypnosis. "I intend to convince you of this in the coming semester."

She looked around the room at the dozen or so students, each, including herself, sitting on a high stool at a drawing table on which there were two large sheets of heavy white paper and a box of pastels. Surely this was the drawing class she'd signed up for, not Psychology 101. What, then, was this man talking about? She sighed, certain that she'd gotten herself into something she was going to regret for the next fifteen weeks.

"You don't need me to teach you how to express yourself," he was saying. "You <u>do</u> need me to teach you basic skills in drawing . . . and seeing. With these skills in hand, you'll be able to release your unique abilities. Now, begin by making two drawings: one of a human head and one of the hand you are <u>not</u> using to draw with."

Jenna thought her drawing of a head resembled an anorexic pumpkin with human features, and the more she worked on it, the worse it looked until she gave up in frustration. But she was able to produce a lifelike image of her left hand, and she became so immersed in it that she gave a start at the touch of a hand on her shoulder. She looked up to see Richard Cayman standing beside her, staring intently at her work.

Up close she saw that his eyes were warmer and far less intimidating than she had first thought. He shifted them to meet hers. "I've never had a student draw the palm before. So unusual. Sorry, you've surprised me. I like that." And a smile as hypnotic as his voice glorified his face. "Please . . . continue—it's really quite good."

With those last four words Jenna took off. Her days were suddenly filled with paper and pastels, and Tuesday and Thursday mornings became the focal points of her week. When the semester ended, she signed up for <u>The World of Water Colors/Mon & Wed 10 a.m./Richard Cayman,MFA.</u>

"Good, yes, I like it! But a touch more green here, don't you think?" Those words and his remarkable smile, and she tumbled down the rabbit's hole. Walking into the supermarket, she hurried to keep up with him, and they discussed what they should do with Jon, their youngest, who refused to eat anything that wasn't peanut butter on white bread. Making the bed, she smiled dreamily, recalling his love-making the night before.

It was hard for her to be objective about her paintings, only seeing them through his eyes. When he leaned close to study one of them and make a comment or suggestion, it was all she could do to lift her brush. The nearness of him, the smell of his after shave paralyzed her. One morning he studied her as well as her painting, saying softly after a long moment, "So . . . luscious. You really have such a special gift."

When especially harried, she found great comfort in his imagined embrace. That he knew nothing of their dream life together didn't deter her. Indeed, it even, as the younger generation said, turned her on.

She came to understand the need to stalk another human being, heretofore a mystery. She longed to know with an intensity out of all proportion to its importance, which of the hundreds of cars in the lot nearest the fine arts building was his, where he put his keys when he got home at night, what kind of music he listened to. And the thought of a real-life wife and children was too painful to entertain.

When she retrieved a scrap of paper from the art room floor one morning, absently glancing at it as she turned to a nearby trash can, her journey through Wonderland took a new turn. The paper was a piece of envelope addressed to Richard: <u>Richard Cayman, 222 West 82nd Street/ Apt.5D, New York, NY 10028.</u> She thrust the scrap deep into the pocket of her skirt and turned slowly to her easel, thoughts in disarray.

"You've put the house on the market? That's crazy, Mom!"

"I've thought it all through," Jenna assured her son. "It's really for the best, dear."

"But what will you do?"

"I'm looking in Manhattan—something on the West Side, I think."

The apartment was dark and seemed incredibly cramped, used as she was to her home's sunny, spacious rooms. There was a moldy smell about it that reminded her of old mushrooms. She followed the realtor into one of the apartment's two bedrooms and pretended to admired the closet the woman pointed out, silently thinking of the off-season clothes she'd have to put into storage. The room was gloomy, its only window facing the neighboring building, but she calculated that the window treatment in her present bedroom could be altered to fit, and it would hide the view.

"You really do need to make a quick decision," the realtor was saying. "I know it sounds like phony sales pressure," she added with a small, apologetic smile, "but it's such a seller's market . . . an apartment like this will disappear in a day or two."

It was on West 83nd Street, one block over from Richard's apartment. She would run into him in Zabar's, the pharmacy, the small café on the corner . . .

With the prospect ahead of her of breaking up a household that had embraced forty years of her life, she decided to forgo a summer course at the college. She pre-registered for one in human figure drawing that Richard would teach in the fall. With that to look forward to, she plunged into the sorting, throwing out, packing, and cleaning that the house required before she could hand it over to the young couple who'd bought it. In addition there were subscriptions to change, services to terminate, utility companies to contact, papers needing her signature. The summer soon became a bog of quicksand, out to suck her under at every turn. Up early and to bed late, her daydream life was her only indulgence.

She had already moved into Manhattan when the closing for the Stelfox house came. Sitting at the lawyer's conference room table, signing the papers required to transfer ownership, she was overcome by confusion and panic. She and Eddie had bought the house during the first year of their marriage. The enormity of what she was doing took her breath away.

Jorge and Lila, the new owners, chatted cheerfully with the lawyers; Jenna felt imprisoned behind the mask that was her face. The screech of pens on the endless papers, Lila's high-pitched giggle, a fly buzzing frantically around a light fixture—all stung her raw, exposed nerves. She got away as quickly as possible, turning down Jorge's invitation to join them for a celebratory lunch.

Labor Day weekend brought with it crisp autumn weather that hung on during the week. On Wednesday Jenna took the car out of the underground garage and inched along city streets thick with morning commuters. The prospect of seeing Richard again had her senses on hyper-alert. The air felt fresher, colors so intense that she pawed through her handbag at the first stall in traffic, searching for sunglasses to cut the glare. When she started across the G W Bridge and heard the sound of the tires, a pleasant zipping noise, she burst into song. Even the discovery of packed parking lots at the college did nothing to dampen her spirits.

The long walk from the far lot where she finally found a space brought her to Richard's classroom a few minutes late to discover a tall woman with fly-away orange hair, wearing a cobalt blue smock, addressing the students. Jenna slid onto a stool behind one of the empty drawing boards and leaned toward the girl seated next to her.

"Where's Richard?" she whispered.

The girl shook her head and pointed at the woman in the smock, who was speaking. ". . . offer came late in August, leaving Richard very little time to pack up and move to Providence in time for RISD's classes to begin. So I'll be your instructor." She swung her head of wild hair to face a boy across the room. "Yes?"

Jenna's head floated free of her body.

The boy's hand hung limply in the air as he asked the woman, "He's not coming back?"

"No," the woman said with exaggerated patience. "Such a long commute from Providence, you know . . ." She rolled her eyes at the rest of the class and was rewarded with nervous laughter. "Now, shall we begin? As I told you, my name is Mamie Oldson, and I'll be your instructor in human . . ."

Jenna didn't stay—couldn't stay. Back in the car, she sat motionless, gripping the steering wheel with shaking hands, the heat of the seat and the enclosed air that pressed against her offering welcome pain that relieved some of the outrage and shock. When the trembling subsided, she opened the windows and drove home.

Thirty-four Stelfox Street sat silent, shuttered against the sun. Lila and Jorge were nowhere to be seen. Jenna stayed in the car and gazed at the house that held all she knew about living. Change is good, she thought, surely it's good. Still she didn't move.

THE END

THE SHINING STAR

"TYLER? JEEZ! What the hell kind of name is that? Sounds like a goddamn last name, not a boy's name!" He shoved his fists into his jacket pockets and glared at the woman in the bed next to the window. She turned her head away, but he knew she was taking it all in—not that he cared. "What's wrong with Jack or Tommy . . . or Mike? Something like that. A real name."

Pattie opened her mouth, but he cut her off.

"Tyler! He'll get the shit beat out of him before he gets to kindergarten!" He watched her face, all blotchy with no makeup, eyes bleary with tears, her lower lip pouted out and shaking, and felt the familiar surge of both shame and gratification that he got whenever he made her cry.

She pressed the remote that hung tied in a loop from the side bar, and the head of the bed went down.

"Okay, so name him Tyler, what the fuck do I care?" He rocked back on his boots. "Look, I gotta go. Hospitals creep me out." He pushed the hair off his forehead with an impatient swipe and took a few backward steps toward the door. "Anyhow, take it easy. You know?"

"Don't you want to hold him?" She waved a hand at the crib, her voice pinched with disappointment.

He looked at the mound of blue swaddled blanket. "No. No, I'd probably drop him. Give you something else to bitch about." He reached the door and turned.

"Call me, Rob. You got to call me, hear? We gotta talk!" Her words followed him into the hall, bouncing off the hard edges of tile.

There was a parking space in front of Dom's Pizzeria, but he cruised on past, the headlights making tunnels in the fog. He knew how it would be: the swoosh of cold air when he pushed Dom's heavy glass door open, and then the hoots and the jokes, because they'd all know by now that Pattie'd had the baby. And everyone knew it was his.

Traffic was building up to rush hour, so he had to sit through two red lights at the intersection by the pond. Too many cars wanting to make left turns held up the rest of them. The woman in the car ahead of him must be going nuts, he thought, because he could see her kids leaping around like a bunch of monkeys. Then they were lined up and leaning over the back seat, staring at him, their foreheads making fat splotches of flesh on the rear window. He gave them the finger and laughed when they startled the mom with their shrieks, silent to him, but probably deafening to her.

Lowering his window, he felt the wet, foggy air on his cheek. It smelled like steam, and he breathed deep gulps of it. The light changed to green. He gunned it, not slowing until he came to Stelfox. As he turned into the driveway, the headlights danced on the reflector his dad had positioned with his usual exacting care.

His mother called to him from the kitchen but, pleading a bad headache, he was able to escape to his room. Sitting down to a meal with her and his dad was nightmare stuff he got out of as often as possible. Their disappointment and disgust were so thick you choked on it. Sometimes they'd look at him, their faces like masks, so you knew they'd rehearsed a bunch of crap about forgiveness, but mostly they'd avert their eyes, look over his shoulder or above his head. He imagined they were still trying to figure it all out: their boy, their shining star, shot down by a wandering sperm.

Only it would've come to nothing if Pattie had been on the pill, like she'd told him she was. He switched on the desk lamp. The fog had turned the windows into two long rectangles of gray flannel, which the lamplight got sucked into, leaving little wattage for the rest of the room. The corners were black holes. The edges of the bookcase blurred, and the shelves receded into darkness, lending them a more interesting appearance, than their usual messy state allowed.

The room was a conglomeration of childhood relics, junior high sports' awards, and teen posters. A grinning Mickey Mouse leaned against a football bearing Joe Montana's autograph. A shoe box full of action figures had overturned, spilling some of them onto the desktop. A battered skateboard contained his cache of <u>Playboy</u> magazines. His mother was always after him to 'weed out,' but he never did.

He threw himself down on the bed and pulled a pillow onto his chest. He inserted a Nirvana CD into the stereo, its insistent beat soon pounding the air and worming its way inside his head. Stupid Pattie, he thought, naming a six-pound kid Tyler. He swung his booted feet to the floor and pushed himself upright. Friggin' kid, he thought.

He shoved the desk chair in front of the bookcase and climbed onto it to reach for the top shelf. A thin veil of dust hit his face as he brought the stuffed bear down. Coughing, he sat down on the chair and whacked the bear sharply against his thigh to get the rest of the dust off it. Gently folding its limbs to its sagging belly, he spilled the remaining action figures from the shoe box and wedged the bear into it. After he had wrapped the box in a paper bag, he took a black marker and, in large letters, wrote, 'TYLER.'

The End

PERILS AND DANGERS

W E SAW ten wild turkeys on our walk this morning. They were wandering as a group, a small herd I suppose you could call them. I've begun to keep track of the wildlife Ozzie and I encounter. We've seen rabbits, an egret on the pond, hawks overhead, and one misty morning deep in the nature center, five deer. The rabbits excite Ozzie and are the reason I keep him on a leash, even though I'd love to see him run loose. I croon, "No bunnies, no bunnies, Oz," and restrain him until the white tails have disappeared in the underbrush. His reaction to the turkeys is different. Perhaps fascinated by their height and stilted movements, he stands frozen. Only his eyes move.

Most mornings when I take Leo his tray of tea and toast, I tell him what we've seen, hoping to stir his interest in the world beyond the four walls of our bedroom. As I open the drapes and raise the shades, I describe the turkeys, how at first I thought they were drab, colorless creatures, but now see their narrow stripes of orange and gold and taupe, muted, understated, beautiful; and how their small, sleek heads and elongated necks remind me of ballerinas. Weaving between and around one another, they seem perfectly choreographed. Unlike the deer, they're never fazed by our presence and regard Ozzie with equanimity.

Leo leans back against the pillows, the tray across his blanketed thighs, and although his eyes, dark luminous stones in a pale face, follow me as I move about, I know his attention is on the plate of whole wheat toast and the cup of green tea that I've served on our best china. He rarely responds.

It was only recently that I learned the truth about his parents. Early in our relationship, during one of those conversations when time flies and suddenly it's daybreak and you have to be at work in a couple of hours, he told me that an aunt and uncle raised him, that his parents were dead. Both claims were true, but like so much that Leo has told me about his past, they were lacking in depth. A banker who dealt with numbers for a living, he became, I suppose, accustomed to the surface, to the black-and-whites of life.

To me, numbers are two-dimensional. They lack the richness of meaning, like notes on a sheet of music which, until voices and instruments take up their story, are flat and without sound. Numbers were the source of our first argument. Argument because that's as far as Leo will go. We've never indulged in a screaming, faces-contorted, emotions-out-of-control, four-letter-word fight. The argument was over the Bloomingdale's bill for furniture I'd purchased. He had seen only the "total amount owed," while I saw his apartment—a monk's quarters before the furniture arrived—transformed into a warm, inviting place to welcome family and friends. In the end we had compromised. I'd sent back an armoire and two lamps, and he'd paid the bill.

Leo's apartment had only one bedroom and a kitchen where, if you stood dead center, you could reach every appliance and nearly every inch of counter space. But the building had a doorman and a round-the-clock desk person and was within walking distance of Leo's office and a short bus ride to mine. The neighborhood, Wall Street, certainly outclassed Jersey City where I had a third floor walk-up. Leo stressed that his place was safe, a point he made repeatedly during our discussions about where we should live. I didn't think much of it at the time.

Have you noticed that life doesn't pay much attention to the expectations or assumptions people have? After 9/11, the apartment, only a couple of blocks from the Trade Center, had an unobstructed view of the smoking aftermath of the terrorists' handiwork. The air, thick with ash whose composition one didn't want to think about, ate at our lungs. The doorman, the round-the-clock desk person—in the crunch they failed Leo. That's how we ended up across the Hudson River in the peaceful suburbs of Northern New Jersey.

I love our house. It's a small cape, painted a cheerful yellow, good roof, more grass than weeds, but it's the street that steals my heart. Turning onto it, huge old trees with low branches meeting overhead make me feel that I've entered an arbor where the filtered light blurs the hard edges. Sidewalks, smooth and darkened with age, provide a perfect surface for children's skates. The houses vary in style, all different yet the same, because they look as though they belong.

At first Leo coped, put on a shirt and tie every morning, and in one of his banker suits he'd drive to the ferry for the trip across the Hudson to Wall Street. But after the holiday break in December, three months after the towers fell, he stopped going into the office. He claimed that he was working from the house, but that pretense didn't stand up when he began to spend most of his days in bed.

Now that we're here, we see my dad more often. He hated the trip into the city and rarely visited us when we lived in the apartment. He likes his son-in-law, but I don't think he knows what to make of Leo's "bump in the road." That's what my dad calls it, a bump in the road. "Everyone hits one at least once in his life, kiddo. Baby him a little, he'll be okay. Watch and see."

I don't tell him how the black cloud that envelops Leo damps down my spirit; how some mornings I want to throw the breakfast tray across the room and shake Leo until I get a reaction, any reaction. I don't tell him how much I miss the old Leo, who used to read me the Sunday comics and laugh harder than I did; how I don't know if he loves me anymore. I never tell my dad these things. I only hope he's right, that Leo's trouble is simply a bump in the road.

Dad's visits bring with them the feeling of normality. The minute he pulls into the driveway in his clunky old Chevy, I feel possibilities opening up. The fact that Leo gets out of bed and puts on a robe, something he does for Dad's visits, is reason enough to lift my spirits. They play chess, Leo on the rocker, Dad across the table from him on the window seat, and while their conversation is sparse, at least it occurs.

Our bed has become Leo's command center. As the days go by, it accumulates: newspapers and books, catalogs and magazines, scrap books and photo albums, CDs and DVDs and tapes—the list seems never-ending. On Saturday mornings while he shaves, I organize the stuff into neat stacks on the floor in order to change the sheets. One rainy Saturday I came across a sleeve of plastic that contained old newspaper articles. As I stood trying to decide which pile to put it on, I glanced at the articles. "PARENTS BUTCHERED WHILE TODDLER LOOKS ON," one announced in bold font. "COUPLE FOUND DEAD; BABY SURVIVES," read another.

From the bathroom I could hear shower water drumming against tiles and glass while an early spring storm carried on outside, the rain beating against the windows with ferocious strength. At first I didn't get it. Poor baby, I thought, putting the plastic sleeve on the miscellaneous pile and turning to strip the bed covers. But even as I began to lament another of life's cruelties, realization spread through my mind like an invasive weed. I went down on my knees and, leaning on shaking hands, read the articles. Dated April 1968, they described how Virginia and Leonard Hulton had been found dead of multiple stab wounds in their home at 1693 Central Avenue, Baltimore, Maryland, and how Virginia's sister, who discovered the bodies, also found little Leonard, her two-year-old nephew, sitting beside his parents' lifeless bodies.

I wrapped my arms around myself and thought about that child, a man now, and realized why safety was the linchpin of his life.

The rabbits and turkeys must be preparing for winter, for we've seen them every morning this past week, watched them searching the tall, wet grasses and underbrush for food. Sweet-tempered Ozzie, trained to be a therapy dog, is a good companion, an animal capable of healing the lonely, the lost, and the abandoned. I have high hopes invested in Ozzie. I watch him as the days bleed into weeks, sitting by the bed, his gentle eyes on Leo's drawn face, silently communicating affection, the embodiment of a safe harbor.

THE END

CROSSING THE STREET

M UCH OF her neighbor Ralph's free time was spent thinking. Nora learned this when she asked him what he was doing, lying there, stretched out on the grassy strip between sidewalk and street in front of his house, one of his arms resting comfortably around the shoulders of his dog. She hadn't asked the obvious question, "Thinking about what?" which, of course, was the information she really sought. Hadn't asked, because the close-up sight of him—she crossed the street so that she didn't have to shout—was always so disquieting. She understood why most passers-by, encountering the two, gave Ralph and the dog a wide berth.

Atwater, and Ralph always used all three syllables when calling him, was the sort of dog who drooled from a perpetually grinning mouth. She supposed he was what was called a mixed breed, but his coat was so unfortunate, that it was hard to determine heritage. Ralph himself wasn't a clean person. His clothes were worn and soiled; his hair, like Atwater's, looked as though it was rarely shampooed. Worn pulled back in a lank, graying ponytail, it wasn't unlike the dog's tail in appearance, if not location. Neither of them was ambitious or industrious—that is, apart from the thinking. When it came to caring for his yard, Ralph obviously embraced the one foot rule—when the grass, which had a multitude of healthy weeds to account for its greenness and vigor, reached a height of one foot, he mowed it. He did spend time on the rusting van of indeterminate color that sat in the driveway, its side reading, "PROFESIONAL PAINTER" and a phone number. The misspelling said it all, Nora thought. However, the van never seemed to profit from his attention.

Surely it was because she considered herself an industrious person that Ralph's habit of lounging for hours on end annoyed her so. Usually she was industrious, although she preferred the word "productive," since this implied a desirable end result to industry. But of late she had to admit to her own periods of inactivity. These also were a source of annoyance, but she rationalized they were the result of her sister's recent death.

Well, not so recent. "It'll be near half a year she's been gone," the cleaning woman had said just yesterday. And there was a word Nora tried to avoid, "gone," like Ronnie was at the grocery store or vacationing in Florida. Strange, the euphemisms people used. "Lost" for instance, as though Nora had misplaced her. A large woman, Ronnie would have been difficult to misplace. "So sorry to hear you lost Ronda" people would say. "Oh, yes," she should reply. "One minute she was here, and the next I couldn't find her." Stupid word, but not nearly as stupid as "passed," she ranted when her other sister Ava told her about the man from down the block having passed. "Not stupid," Ava declared, "actually rather poetic, from the phrase 'passed away.' So much gentler than 'died.'

"But I haven't come to discuss semantics with you." Ava fixed her with her school-teacher glare. "What are you doing, Nora? No, don't answer that, we all know what you're doing—nothing! You sit around here sighing and napping, napping and sighing. You've dropped out of every activity and club you used to participate in, you don't return phone calls or answer e-mails. I bet you don't even use the computer, do you?" Ava went on and on about Nora's shortcomings. Nora let her run through the whole list.

She was in the habit of tuning Ava out. Instead she considered the boxwood hedge visible through the front window, dismayed that it had gotten so out of shape, so in need of clipping. But were she to approach the hedge with clippers, Ralph and Atwater would untangle their limbs and rise, to cross the street, Ralph to offer advice, Atwater to lift his leg and urinate a long killing stream on the defenseless branches. She wouldn't be terribly surprised if they would materialize were she to creep out at night in the light of the street lamp to do the pruning. She had past experience with Ralph advising her. And since he'd taken to this thinking thing, lying there on the grass for hours on end, she didn't have a hope of avoiding him. It was unfortunate that Ralph considered himself a gardener.

As she watched Ava's mouth, giving no thought to the words spilling out of it, she considered how long she'd stared at Ava's thin lips and flashing tongue. Nora had developed the habit in childhood, when Ava, five years her senior, took it upon herself to play mother, a stern, humorless mother. Ronnie, only a year younger than Ava, had slipped under her radar.

"Nora!" Ava cried. "You're not listening! You have that dopey look on your face, with your mind a thousand miles away, thinking about something else. That is, if you're even thinking." She gathered up her sweater and handbag, then put them down, as she remembered something. "What is that man doing? You know, who I mean, that awful neighbor with the vicious dog. You'll never be able to sell this house with him lying over there like some sort of dead corpse. And what about that truck?" Ava continued. "It's been parked there forever."

"Actually, in this town it's illegal," Nora said absently. What was Ava talking about, selling the house? Nora wasn't selling. But there was no reasoning with her sister, once she was on a tear. Otherwise, to her own surprise, she would have come to Ralph's defense, because Atwater wasn't vicious.

After Ava finally left, Nora wandered through the rooms she'd occupied since childhood. With the exception of the few years she'd lived in an apartment, these rooms had been her only home. Now she walked through them with the thought that Ava had planted in her mind. Had the time really come for her to find a smaller place? She, Ronnie, and Ava had grown up in the house. Ronnie had never left it, while Nora had lived her married years in a city apartment until her husband had died an early death. After burying him, she moved home. She'd lived longer with Ronnie than with her husband.

Through a window in what had been Ronnie's bedroom, she looked down on Ralph and Atwater lying in the rosy, slanted rays of the late afternoon sun. Ralph and his wife Pearl, who rarely appeared and who Nora suspected of being mentally challenged, were misfits on Stelfox Street. It was Pearl who'd inherited their house, a fifties split level, left to her by her grandmother, Nora had heard, a bit of neighborhood gossip, but probably true. The house was as disheveled as Ralph and Atwater and stood out on Stelfox, where houses were of the large, front porch sort, kept in, if not immaculate, then at least cared-for condition.

Yet it had been Ralph who Nora had turned to when she needed help getting Ronnie to various doctors. Her bedroom had always been Ronnie's favorite spot in the house. As a child she'd played in it for hours, shunning the opportunities to play outdoors with her sisters and the neighborhood children. It was there that she'd increasingly spent her days until, toward the end, she'd been unable to leave it. Ronnie, chubby as a child, and what was euphemistically called "heavy" as an adult, was obese in her later years—obese and beautiful, her skin smooth and fresh, her voice clear, lacking the huskiness that often dogged the elderly.

Trips became for Ronnie the few steps across the hall to the bathroom. Otherwise, her days were spent in a super-wide recliner Nora and Ava had found at the Laz-E-Boy store, with an afternoon nap on the bed. Of course, there was television, and always the phone, Ronnie's connection to life beyond the bedroom. Nora had tried to interest her in using the computer, with the wide world it offered, but Ronnie had a real love for the phone. She liked holding on to people, knowing they were connected to her at the other end of the line. Her voice, child-like in its sweetness and phrasing, had been the background Nora had lived with for years.

It was only in the last month or so of Ronnie's life that the quiet waters had been disturbed, and it had become necessary for her to face the prospect of steps and cars. Nora and even a huskier Ava, weren't up to the task. Hilly, Ava's husband, had a bad back with discs that had ruptured in the past, and was unable to help. The sisters' friends were in similar circumstances—vulnerable hips, heart conditions, replaced knees. That was when Nora had approached Ralph about assisting her sister.

He'd been quick to sign on for the job, refusing to take any sort of payment Nora repeatedly offered. And he'd been surprisingly gentle, patient with Ronnie's fear of falling, fixed and unshakable as they navigated steps. Nora had been embarrassed having him—a large man who filled too much of available space with body and clothes that were days old—accompany them into doctors' waiting rooms. It was a reaction she regretted, but hadn't been able to shake. With one part of her, she'd wanted to explain to the clean, neatly-dressed patients who looked at Ralph with curiosity and usually disapproval, that he wasn't related to Ronnie and her. Yet with another part, the better part, she thought, she'd wanted to defend him for the service he was giving generously and freely.

Nora found she wasn't hungry for dinner, a soft boiled egg and piece of rye toast sufficing. Nights without Ronnie were lonely and too still, even with the television droning. By ten, Nora was in bed, if not asleep, for Ava's mention of selling the house, like a pea under the mattress, caused her thoughts to drift here and there. Even the soft patter of rain on the windows failed to soothe her, and it wasn't until dawn that the mourning dove's insistent call lulled her into a deep sleep. It was after ten before she woke to the phone ringing.

"So what d'you think?" Ava began the conversation.

"I don't know . . . think about what? Is it raining?"

"Forget the rain. Is the truck gone?"

Nora struggled out of the warm clutch of the covers. "Ava, what's wrong with you? What are you talking about? What truck?"

"That horrible truck he keeps in the driveway . . . your stupid neighbor, what's his name? Ralph? Is it gone? The truck, I mean."

Nora padded barefoot across the room to the window. Raising the shade, she squinted in strong sunlight until she was able to see the driveway in question. There was no familiar van. "Yeah . . . it _is_ gone. How'd you know that?"

Ava's laugh hurt Nora's ear. "I called your town hall and reported it to the police. You were right, there's a town statute that makes it illegal to park a commercial vehicle on private property. Seems they told him to move it, and he got real nasty, so they said they towed it. I just called them. They thanked me. So what d'you think? Now it'll be a lot easier to sell the house. What we should do is . . ."

Nora stopped listening. Before she'd only heard and read the expression about having one's breath taken away, but that was exactly how Ava's news had struck her. Once her breathing was restored, she returned the phone to its cradle, silencing Ava.

By noon the sun had dried the grass that had been drenched during the night, but Ralph and Atwater didn't appear, and their thinking spot remained unoccupied. As Ava had described, Nora spent the day napping and sighing, although she found herself, like her neighbor, also doing a lot of thinking.

THE END

THIS IS NOT A PARTY

"THE DOCTORS told her that her body won't tolerate any more chemo or radiation." Jane paused before adding, "And she's been turned down for the bone marrow transplant."

Kate could hear a catch in her sister's breathing. "Oh . . . so . . . we're talking dying, aren't we? I mean, she's . . . is that what you're hearing?"

"Yeah . . . it is. Bob said she'll be in the hospital's hospice program."

"How is Bob?"

"You know our brother; not a lot of communication going on there."

"True, but remember all the stress he's handled. And he's always there for her."

"He is, but he's carrying stoicism too far. He's going to cave in, collapse under the weight of it all."

"I know. We've talked about all this before, and it gets us nowhere." Kate turned the pages of her weekly calendar book. "How old is Jossie? Do you know?"

"In her late forties, isn't she? Yes, she's forty-nine; she's two years older than me."

"God, that's too young." Kate studied the calendar. "Okay, look, it's the middle of August. Chuck is traveling so much, he'll hardly notice I'm gone, and Thad can fend for himself, so I think I'll drive down on Tuesday. We can split the months. I'll stay with her the first two weeks, you take the second two. That way, Bob won't have to hire someone, some stranger, to be with her."

After she'd said good-bye to her sister and replaced the receiver, she sat for a moment gazing out at the sun glinting off the pool. The dog stirred at her feet, his sorrowful spaniel eyes on her face. "What's wrong, McGee?

You heard me make travel plans?" He wedged his solid head into her lap, and her fingers began to massage his velvet ears and broad head. But it was Jossie's head she was seeing, resting on a hospital pillow, as Kate had bent over to kiss her good bye the previous April—Jossie's head, bare of all but a few wispy strands of colorless hair. She finished the dog's massage with a pat on his head. "You're a good boy, McGee. I won't be gone long, and Thad'll be here with you."

That evening, after a long phone conversation with her husband, who was in Los Angeles on business, Kate brewed a pot of coffee and, hearing her son descending from the second floor, set out two mugs.

"Let's have our coffee in the family room," she said. "I feel like I've been in this kitchen all day."

They settled into worn, comfortable chairs, and Thad reached over and turned on the radio. The slow, deliberate beat of a jazz quartet filled the room. "Perfect," he said. "This'll drive away all thoughts of job applications and interviews."

"Hard on the ego after four years of academia, hmm?" She rubbed a hand under the bottom of the mug of coffee. "I'm going to New Jersey in a day or two, going to leave McGee and the house for you to take care of. Be okay?"

"Sure. Going to see Granddad?"

"Yes, and spend my days with Aunt Jossie. She's been in the hospital, and she's going to need lots of help when she gets home."

He rolled his eyes. "She's always in the hospital."

Kate sighed. Thad had probably been only nine or ten when his aunt was first diagnosed with lymphoma. Joss had always shared every new development of her and Bob's health with the family, but when she discovered that first lump in her neck, her medical bulletins, as Chuck called them, had left poison ivy and bronchitis far behind and entered the dark, scary territory of tumors, depleted red blood cells, and deep radiation. "Her doctor's put her in a hospice program."

"Oh," he said, looking surprised. "You mean . . . she's dying?"

Over the years, Kate had envisioned the cancer flailing away at Joss's body, only to see her stand up, brush herself off, and check the kitchen shelves to see what was needed at the supermarket. Life went on. Until now. "Well, things don't look so good for her."

Thad shook his head. "Life sure is one hell of a party." Rising, he leaned over, and, kissing the top of her head, said, "Mom, don't die 'til you're a little old, pain-in-the-ass lady." He picked up the empty mugs and headed for the kitchen.

When Kate pulled into her father's driveway, he was on the front porch of his small house, his fingertips testing a flowerbox for moisture. He came carefully down the steps, holding the handrail with one pale, blue-veined hand, and she felt the momentary shock that always assailed her when she first saw him after a few months' interval.

"Earlier than I expected, Kate," he greeted her, his voice stronger than his frail frame suggested.

"Early start, Dad. How are you?" She kissed his cool, wrinkled cheek.

"Fine, just fine." He reached for the case she was lifting from the trunk. "And the cats?"

"As regal and demanding as ever." He started up the steps, then turned to her. "Guess you know Jocelyn's in the hospital."

"Yes—Jane told me."

"Awful thing." He shook his head, and she could see tears swamp his faded blue eyes.

She called Jossie that evening, thinking as she dialed the hospital number of how often her calls to her sister-in-law were made with Dread perched on her shoulder and Duty pushing her from behind. She sat holding the receiver to her ear, listening to the rings, aware and discomfited by her own good health, by being able to look ahead to another year.

"Hello?" Jossie's voice sounded faint but cheerful.

"It's Kate, Jossie. Do I have you at a bad time?"

"No, it's okay. How are you, honey?"

"I'm good—a little stiff from the drive, but good. What about you? You sound stronger than when we talked last week. They're taking good care of you?"

"Yeees." She drew the word out. Never a fast talker, she was speaking even slower than she usually did. "I think I can go home tomorrow. I have to agree to go by ambulance—and let Bob order a hospital bed."

"Okay . . . that seems reasonable—you'll be more comfortable."

"I guess so. I'm glad you're here, Kate."

"Me, too. I'm eager to see you."

"Maybe tomorrow." She paused, and Kate could hear the sounds of a television game show in the background. "Bob was here," she continued. "This afternoon . . . when the doctors came in. Dr. Swan told us the

Interferon might buy me some time, but that the cancer was spreading, which is why I'm so weak. It was good Bob was here . . . so he understands my situation."

Was it the medication? Kate wondered. Jossie had delivered the words like the voice on the recording at the local theater, announcing names and times of coming attractions. Kate stared at frolicking cat magnets securing a store list, photos, even a sequined calendar, to the refrigerator door. She could hear blood pounding past her ears.

"Don't you agree?" Jossie asked.

"Yes . . . I guess you're right."

"Did I have my tea?"

"You did, Joss, but maybe you'd like another cup." Kate put down her knitting and went over to the bed.

"No, no more." Her eyelids drifted shut, and she lay still under a light blanket.

Kate picked up her knitting but sat with it idle in her hands and instead watched plump birds fluttering in a thicket of shrubs outside the bedroom windows. Perched on fragile branches, they were pecking at hundreds of orange berries growing on one of the bushes. As the September days slipped away, the leaves were taking on a golden sheen that the afternoon sun intensified and reflected, casting the light into the bedroom. Dipping and pecking, the birds peered in at the two women. We must seem a picture of indolence, Kate thought; day after day, Jossie in bed, me in this chair. They have no idea how hard we're working.

In the kitchen Kate did all the myriad deft and purposeful things that Jossie, given good health, would have been doing for herself. She wondered if, from her hospital bed down the hall, Jossie could hear her opening the refrigerator, running water, rattling cutlery. She wondered, were their roles reversed, if she could have borne the depth of loss those kitchen sounds represented.

Bob came home as each day wound down, always managing a smile and bringing into the still house trails of vitality. Then Kate kissed Jossie's cheek and, after conferring with her brother about the day and the meal she'd prepared for him, got into her car and drove to her father's house until the following morning, when she returned. She tried not to think too much about her brother's current life.

The brilliant days of October came and went, dying in the ominous chill of early November. Winter stalked, devouring the light, and Kate wakened in blue darkness to hurry through her morning ritual in order to reach the home on Stelfox Street before Bob had to leave for the city.

From her chair she watched Jossie sleep whole days away, her body occasionally twitching but otherwise motionless. Wakened for doses of the liquid morphine that Kate took from a refrigerator shelf, a gorgeous turquoise that belied its purpose, Jossie often mistook her and the bedroom for her dream. Kate sat, and one afternoon watched the leaves fill the air outside the window, cutting off the light as they fell, as though they'd all realized of a sudden that they'd overstayed their welcome. She listened to the house noises—vents creaking as drafts of hot air issued from the furnace, the wired hum of the refrigerator from the kitchen, the occasional drip of a faucet, everything but the soft whish of Jossie's breathing. Yet when she looked at her lying behind the metal bars of the bed, she saw the nearly imperceptible rise and fall of the quilt over her chest, and her covered leg twitching gently down its length.

THE END